Adam looked up into the pale blue eyes of the mother of all those children.

"Thank you," she murmured, her voice clear despite all the confusion around them.

"No problem," he ground out between more coughing.

"Do you always do that?" Carly asked.

"Do what?"

She crouched beside his stretcher. "Deflect a compliment. I was thanking you for saving my son from the fire. And Molly. What you did was extraordinarily brave. I don't know how I can ever repay you."

He gave her a tiny salute and muttered, "All in the line of work," then lay back down. Molly the dog was lying on the stretcher beside his, apparently playing dead except that her tail was wagging.

Adam closed his eyes.

Dear Reader,

I'm delighted to bring you the fourth book of The O'Malley Men series, which is also a Creature Comforts title.

Many of my readers have been intrigued by youngest brother, Adam, the firefighter. He's been an enigmatic figure in my previous books, *Colorado Christmas, The Sheriff and the Baby* and *Colorado Cowboy*, drifting in and out of family gatherings, never really connecting with anyone.

So, to make Adam reveal his true self, I've had him move back to his hometown of Spruce Lake. Only problem is, moving back to the town he escaped when barely out of his teens has forced Adam to confront the demons from his past.

Adam is good at pretending that nothing touches him, but he's a dedicated firefighter. Hailed a hometown hero when he saves both a toddler and a dog from a burning building, Adam tries to shy away from the accolades, knowing he's no hero. Instead, he's been harboring a dreadful secret and he's convinced that when the town discovers the truth, he'll be condemned instead of praised.

But of course the large and gregarious O'Malley clan isn't letting Adam hide from either them or his past. Add to the mix the mother of the toddler, Carly Spencer, who refuses to let Adam get under her skin.

Adam is in for the ride of his life with Carly, her four children, his matchmaking mother and Molly the basset hound.

I love hearing from readers. You can email me at cc@cccoburn.com. Please watch for the fifth and final installment of The O'Malley Men, when we finally learn why Jack left the seminary to become a master carpenter— and when an old flame comes to Spruce Lake and turns his life upside down.

Happy reading and healthy lives!
C.C. Coburn

Colorado Fireman

C.C. COBURN

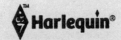

TORONTO NEW YORK LONDON
AMSTERDAM PARIS SYDNEY HAMBURG
STOCKHOLM ATHENS TOKYO MILAN MADRID
PRAGUE WARSAW BUDAPEST AUCKLAND

Recycling programs
for this product may
not exist in your area.

ISBN-13: 978-0-373-75399-4

COLORADO FIREMAN

Copyright © 2012 by Catherine Cockburn

ABOUT THE AUTHOR

C.C. Coburn married the first man who asked her and hasn't regretted a day since—well, not many of them. She grew up in Australia's Outback, moved to its sun-drenched Pacific coast, then traveled the world. A keen skier, she discovered Colorado's majestic Rocky Mountains and now divides her time between Australia and Colorado. Home will always be Australia, where she lives with her husband and two of her three grown children (the third having recently moved to England), as well as a Labrador retriever and three cats. But her heart and soul are firmly planted in Colorado, too. Her books have received glowing reviews and a number of awards. She loves hearing from readers; you can visit her at www.cccoburn.com.

Books by C.C. Coburn
HARLEQUIN AMERICAN ROMANCE
1283—COLORADO CHRISTMAS
1309—THE SHERIFF AND THE BABY
1337—COLORADO COWBOY

All backlist available in ebook. Don't miss any of our special offers. Write to us at the following address for information on our newest releases.

Harlequin Reader Service
U.S.: 3010 Walden Ave., P.O. Box 1325, Buffalo, NY 14269
Canadian: P.O. Box 609, Fort Erie, Ont. L2A 5X3

Many thanks to

Battalion Chief Neil "Rosie" Rosenberger and
Captain Derek "Goose" Goossen of the Red,
White and Blue for their invaluable assistance and
patience with my research. It's encouraging to know
our safety is in the hands of such capable men.

Remedial massage therapist Lynn Creighton for
her help and insights into what is involved in
massage therapy and for her amazing massages.

And my dear friends, equine veterinarian
Dr. Holly Wendell and horse-rescuer Helen Lacey
for again patiently educating me about horses.

Any errors or discrepancies in this story are the
fault of the author and in no way reflect the
expertise of the aforementioned.

Chapter One

Desperate for more air, Firefighter Adam O'Malley cracked open the bypass on the regulator leading to his airpack.

The smoke inside the apartment building in Spruce Lake, Colorado, was thick and filled with lethal fumes. His helmet light shone through the gloom, barely illuminating his path as combustible materials manufactured in the seventies ensured the building burned fast and hot. Thankfully, the positive pressure inside his face mask prevented the noxious wastes from entering through its seals.

Adam heard the unmistakable whimper of a child and turned toward it.

He'd promised the mother he'd bring her toddler out alive. His vow had been the only thing that kept her from racing into the burning building to save her son.

Adam hadn't lost a victim yet and today wasn't going to be his first, not if he could help it.

Dropping to all fours, he crawled along the floor, where the smoke was less thick, toward the child. He spotted the little guy because of his diaper, a white beacon in an otherwise blackened world. He was on the floor beside his crib, hands stretched out, tears running down his chubby cheeks.

How could anyone have left a kid behind? he wondered

as he ripped open his bunker coat, lifted the child into his arms and placed him inside its protection, talking to him in soothing tones. "It's okay, little guy. I've got you now. We'll see your mom in no time," he assured the child, praying their exit hadn't been blocked by falling beams or other debris.

He picked his way back out of the apartment, his body and jacket shielding the boy who clung to him, whimpering. The deafening sounds of fire consuming everything in its path—timber splintering, walls exploding, windows shattering—followed Adam as he moved down the stairs, testing each step to ensure it was still intact. Moments later, they were outside in the bright winter sunshine.

The child's mother broke from Captain Martin Bourne's hold and rushed toward them. Tears streaming down her face, she muttered incoherently as she tried to take the child from his arms. But Adam wasn't giving up his charge just yet. The paramedics needed to check him over, so he grabbed her with his free hand and directed her to the ambulances waiting nearby.

He'd just extracted the child's deathlike grasp around his neck when the mother screamed and raced back toward the building.

"Don't tell me she's got *another* kid!" Adam yelled at his captain as he ran to intercept the woman.

Then he noticed she was chasing after one of the kids they'd rescued earlier. He was running back into the building. What was it with this family?

Adam had always been quick on his feet, and in spite of the cumbersome firefighting gear he wore, he managed to overtake the mother, warning her to "Get back!" as he passed her.

He caught up with the kid, threw him over his shoulder in a fireman's hold and returned to where Martin was trying to calm the mother. The kid kicked and screamed and beat at Adam's back but the blows slid off his bunker jacket, slick with water from the fire hoses.

He put the kid down but the boy spun away, intent on running into the building. Adam reached out one arm, snagged the child and hunkered down in front of him.

"What do you think you're doing, son? We got all your family out," he said.

"M…M…Molly's in there."

Adam glanced up at the mother. "You've got *another* kid?" Sheesh, how many did this woman have? Four frightened children had been extracted from the building and she looked as if she was hardly out of her teens.

"Tiffany was babysitting my children," the mother explained. "She got my oldest *three* children out."

Served him right for making that comment about her having another kid.

"Molly is the Polinskis' dog," she said.

"How do you know she isn't already out?"

The woman indicated two elderly people being loaded into ambulances. "They'd never go anywhere without Molly."

Except from a burning building, Adam wanted to say.

"Mrs. Polinski told me she's still inside!" the child yelled over the sound of more parts of the building collapsing. "She wants me to get her!"

Adam closed his eyes. Some days he hated his job. There was no way he'd find the poor animal. Not until long after the fire was out…

"Son, it's too late to get her," Adam said in as soothing a voice as he could muster. What the hell were the old people thinking? Expecting a kid to go rescue their dog?

As if reading his mind, a hound of some kind howled

mournfully. Another of the woman's children screamed, this one a girl of about six. "Please! Get Molly!" she cried.

Adam wished everyone would calm down and stop yelling.

"Which apartment is she in?" he asked as the dog continued to howl.

The woman pointed up to the third floor. "The one on the end, next to ours."

Adam looked into the eyes of his battalion chief and knew he was going to refuse.

"Wait till the ladder truck gets here. We'll reassess the situation then," Chief Malone said.

Adam released the boy and stood. "You know I can't leave her there, Chief," he said and, without waiting for his go-ahead, turned back toward the building.

His battalion chief's warning shout ringing in his ears, Adam sprinted up the stairs to the third level. As he did, they collapsed beneath him. He leaped the last couple of steps and landed heavily on his face, smashing his face mask and breaking the connection to his air supply. The mask filled with acrid smoke.

Ripping it off, Adam crouched down and crawled toward the sound of a dog scratching frantically on the other side of a door at the end of the hall. Adam had no idea how people could leave their precious pets behind in a fire. Or any other disaster, for that matter.

Coughing because of the smoke, he opened the door.

Inside, he found the saddest-looking dog in the world. Without wasting a second, he scooped up the basset hound, headed across the room to the window and kicked through it.

As the glass shattered onto the snow-covered ground below, he gulped fresh air into his lungs. "Ladder!" he yelled, but his voice was a harsh squawk.

Since the stairs had collapsed, the ladder truck was their only way out of the building. If it hadn't arrived, he and Molly were toast. Literally.

Irritated by the smoke, he blinked, forcing his eyes to water. A shout came from below as someone spotted him. Adam waited and prayed, sucking in huge lungfuls of air. Finally, the truck swung its ladder around toward him.

The terrified young dog squirmed in his arms. "Easy, girl," he murmured as he swung his leg out over the ledge and waited until the bucket attached to the ladder was within reach.

The smoke billowing out of the window behind him was growing thicker, choking him and the dog, who was now squirming and coughing so much he could barely hold her. He glanced back to see flames licking through the apartment's doorway. The entire building was in imminent danger of collapse.

The bucket finally reached Adam's precarious ledge and he stepped into it. "Everything's okay, girl," he said as they cleared the building. "We'll have you down in a moment."

His tone seemed to calm her and she settled in his arms, whimpering softly as they were lowered to the ground.

Once there, he was immediately surrounded by other firefighters. Molly licked his face. That small act of gratitude drained the tension of the past few desperate minutes from Adam's body. He smiled and ruffled her ears. She was grubby with soot, and the soot covering the gloved hand he was petting her with wasn't helping but he was too spent to pull off his gloves.

Exhausted, he allowed Martin Bourne to take her from his arms, then fell onto the stretcher under a triage tent set up by the EMT who was attached to their firehouse. After she'd placed an oxygen mask over his nose and mouth, she fitted another one on Molly, who lay on a stretcher beside him.

The dog was coughing pretty badly. "Look after her," Adam croaked, pushing the EMT's hand away as she began to wash out his burning eyes.

She ignored him and continued squeezing liquid into his eyes, then checked his vitals. He closed his eyes against the pain in his lungs and tried to relax in spite of his still-racing heart.

The flash from a camera bored through his eyelids. He looked up into the lens of Ken Piper, photographer for the local paper. "How does it feel to be a hero, Adam?" he asked.

Adam grunted.

"How about one of you and the dog? Smile!" Molly was lying on her back, all four legs in the air. She'd stopped coughing, so it was hard to tell if she was dead, playing dead or wanted her tummy rubbed. Ken's camera flashed again, then he melted into the crowd.

"Adam!" Hearing the familiar sound of his mother's voice, he opened his eyes again. Sure enough, his mom was elbowing her way through the crowd gathered around him and Molly.

He felt about twelve years old as he looked into his mom's piercing blue eyes and she glared down at him.

Positive that he was in for a lecture, he offered her a sheepish grin. "I got her out," he said, reaching across to rub Molly's tummy, hoping his mom would go easy on him since she was an animal lover. He didn't need a dressing-down in front of everyone.

"You sure did, darling," Sarah said, and dropped to her knees beside Adam and threw her arms around him. "I've never seen anything braver in my life."

She hugged him so fiercely the air whooshed out of his lungs, which started a coughing jag that felt as if daggers had been plunged into his chest.

"Careful, Mrs. O'Malley," his captain said. "Your son's just saved a baby, an elderly woman and a dog. Give him breathing room. There's little enough oxygen at this altitude as it is."

His mom drew back and cupped his cheek, making Adam feel like an eight-year-old instead. Why didn't she do this to any of his other brothers? Being the youngest of five boys was a curse. Since he was about to turn thirty, you'd think she'd accept that he was an adult now.

His mother's voice shook as she said, "I've never been prouder of any of my sons than I am today." Then she burst into tears.

Adam didn't know what to do. His mother rarely let her emotions show—except when she was really angry—but now she was in all-out blubbering mode.

Luckily, Martin was good at dealing with emotional women and led his mom away, shouting over his shoulder at his men, "Find out if there's a veterinarian in the crowd to check out that dog."

Adam rubbed his eyes, unsure if his vision was blurred by the smoke or by his reaction to his mom's emotional display. Guaranteed, she'd be talking about this for a few years to come.

He'd been back in Spruce Lake less than a week and he'd had to fight his first big fire.

And then his mom had shown up. Great! Just great.

One of the reasons Adam had postponed returning to his hometown to fight fires was because of this very situation. He didn't want any of his family seeing the risks he took. His brother Matt, the county sheriff, knew full well the dangers of firefighting, but Adam had always played down the risks when discussing his job with his family.

There was another reason he'd stayed away from Spruce Lake. The reason he'd spent half his life trying to run from his hometown. Someday soon, he needed to confront that.

Adam rubbed his eyes again and started to sit up. He needed to get out of there, but found himself pushed back down as the paramedic washed out his eyes again. "I'm fine," he protested.

"I decide when you're fine," she said, placing the oxygen mask over his face again. "Breathe," she commanded. "I'll be back in a minute. I've got other firefighters to see. It's not all about you, Adam—you dog-rescuer, you." He could hear the gentle sarcasm in her voice.

"Don't hurry back," he muttered, and closed his eyes, breathing in the cool air, feeling it surge into his lungs, restoring the O2 levels to his bloodstream. He coughed again and sat up, then removed his mask and coughed up black goop that had gotten into his lungs. He spat it out.

Only it landed on a pair of white sneakers. He looked up into the pale blue eyes of the mother of all those children.

"Thank you," she murmured.

"No problem," he gasped between more coughing. "Anything else you want me to spit on?"

"Do you always do that?" she asked.

"Do what?"

She crouched beside him. "Deflect a compliment. I was thanking you for saving my son. And Molly. What you did was extraordinarily brave. I don't know how I can ever repay you."

He gave her a tiny salute, muttered, "All in the line of work," and lay back down. He didn't want to talk to this woman. To anyone. He wanted a long shower and clean sheets. *Cool,* clean sheets.

CARLY SPENCER STOOD for a moment watching the fire-fighter who'd saved her son Charlie's life, knowing he'd shut his eyes to get rid of her.

She'd wept as he carried Charlie out of the burning building. She'd been so sure he wouldn't be found. Jessica, the babysitter she'd hired to care for her children after school, had been sick today and sent a friend to fill in for her.

Since today, the last day of school before the February break, had been declared a snow day, although the weather had turned unexpectedly mild, so it was actually more of a slush day, her three oldest children were home. And since Carly had back-to-back massage appointments booked at the Spruce Lodge spa—and God knew, she needed the money—she'd had to get moving and hadn't taken enough time to run through the children's routines with Tiffany. The girl had obviously panicked and forgotten all about eighteen-month-old Charlie sleeping in the bedroom that was farthest from the living room.

"I'm so sorry, Mrs. Spencer!" she'd cried as Carly pulled up in her vehicle in front of the burning building. "There was this huge explosion and all I could think about was getting the kids out.... But then when we got down here, I remembered the baby was sleeping in the back room."

Her words had sliced into Carly's heart. Without hesitating, she'd raced into the building and collided with a firefighter who was coming out with Mrs. Polinski in his arms.

He'd handed the old woman to a colleague and grabbed Carly by the arms.

"You're not going in there!" he'd yelled through his mask.

"My baby's inside!" she screamed. "I have to get him out!"

"Which floor?"

"Third. First door on your right!"

The words had scarcely left her mouth when he released her and ran back into the building as another firefighter carried Mr. Polinski outside.

Someone grasped her by the shoulders. "Come over here away from the danger, ma'am," he said. "Adam will find your baby."

The man seemed confident of Adam's ability to find one tiny little boy in a huge inferno, but the sound of the building disintegrating and the amount of smoke billowing from the windows and doorways eroded her hope that the firefighter would get to Charlie in time.

Alex, Jake and Maddy had huddled around her, trembling with fear and shock. Carly hugged them close and waited.

She'd felt a prickle of apprehension go up her spine—as if someone was watching her. She glanced around at the crowd. *Of course people are watching you,* she chastised herself. Still, the sensation was so weird…. She searched the faces, but saw no one familiar. Shrugging it off, she put it down to her fears for Charlie.

When the firefighter returned, holding Charlie protectively beneath his coat, she'd rushed to take her son from him.

But then Alex had raced back toward the building to find Molly. Carly hadn't had time to wonder about the Polinskis leaving her behind; maybe everything had happened too quickly for anyone to think rationally. The fact that her babysitter had left Charlie behind was evidence enough of that.

The firefighter had charged into the building to rescue Molly. Carly had held her breath, fearing for his and Molly's lives. And then she'd heard the glass shattering as he'd kicked out the window. The smoke was so thick as it poured out of the window that she couldn't see him clearly. But Carly knew without a doubt it was the heroic firefighter who'd saved her son, and now he'd saved Molly.

She'd needed to thank him and had waited until he'd been checked out by the EMT before approaching. But then an older woman had come by and made a fuss over him. She'd soon realized the woman was his mom. And she was annoying her son. Carly smiled. She would've acted in exactly the same way had it been one of her children who'd acted so fearlessly.

"ADAM? WHAT THE…?"

He opened one eye to find Dr. Lucy Cochrane on the other side of the stretcher.

Lucy knelt beside him, opened his jacket and put her stethoscope to his chest. The EMT had already checked his signs and was now working on some of his colleagues. Adam didn't have the energy to point that out to Lucy so he let her examine him. She was an old school buddy of his brother Matt's. Bossy, but a good friend to the family. And if Lucy was around, the woman with too many kids might leave him alone. She made him uncomfortable.

Made him yearn for things he'd denied himself for too long.

"I heard you'd come back to town. Just as well, or that dog might not have survived. Brave boy." She patted his cheek.

Adam resisted the urge to groan. His older brothers' friends still acted like he was a kid. And they all wondered why he couldn't wait to get out of town once he'd finished high school. If they'd known the truth, they sure wouldn't think he was so heroic.

Lucy listened to his chest and nodded. "Keep breathing," she said, and put the mask back on his face.

"Thanks. I intend to," Adam said with a note of gentle sarcasm as Lucy did a thorough exam under the watchful eyes of the toddler's mother. He thought again that she looked way too young to have so many kids. She resembled Meg Ryan—skinny legs, flyaway blond hair—and she seemed so vulnerable that Adam experienced an unwanted but overwhelming urge to protect her.

He wondered where all her kids were now. Had she managed to misplace one of them again? And where exactly was her husband?

Lucy departed with a promise to return again soon. Adam closed his eyes, then jumped as something wet and slimy collided with his cheek. He opened his eyes. Louella, Mayor Frank Farquar's pet pig, was standing over him. He wiped the slobber with the back of his hand. What the hell was Louella doing at a fire?

She grunted at him and went to shove her snout against his face again, but Adam pulled away in time. That was when he noticed Louella's feet. She was wearing bright red rubber booties.

"What the hell?"

"Who knew old Lou doesn't like the feel of snow between her dear little trotters?" his brother Will said from behind Louella.

"A pig in rubber boots. Now I've seen everything," Adam said. Could this day get any weirder?

"You did good, little brother," Will told him. "Lou was only showing her appreciation."

Adam groaned. Will and Louella had, in Adam's opinion, an unnatural relationship. Will didn't mind hanging out with Louella and, stranger still, she didn't mind hanging out with him.

He and Will were opposites. Will loved everyone and they all loved him. So did their animals. Adam had always found social situations difficult and preferred his own company, much like his older brother Luke, who ran the family ranch.

A camera flash went off in his face just as Louella swooped in again. "You put that in the paper, Ken, and you're dead," Adam growled through clenched teeth.

"Hey, your ugly mug will be all over the paper tomorrow," Ken said. "Human interest, you know."

"Or porcine…" Will said with a grin.

"Go away. Both of you," Adam said. "And take her with you."

"Come on, Lou. I'm sure we can find someone who appreciates your affectionate advances."

Adam watched as Louella trotted off behind Will, her bright red boots contrasting with the snow. She paused and glanced back at him. "Don't even think about it!"

Louella snorted and turned to follow Will.

"Darling!"

It was his mom again. Adam sighed. "Spare me from women," he begged skyward.

"You don't like women?" the mother with too many kids asked. She was holding one of her kids—the toddler he'd rescued. He was perched on her hip, but looked way too heavy for someone as small as her to be carrying around.

"He comes from a family of brothers," his mother said, completely ignoring the fact that Adam was about to answer for himself. "Unfortunately, he doesn't relate to the opposite sex very well." She offered her hand to the woman. "I'm Sarah O'Malley, by the way."

Adam wasn't about to tell her he related perfectly well to women. Just not to bossy ones. Like his mom. And Lucy. And now this nosy woman with black spit all over her sneakers.

"Carly Spencer," the woman said, giving her own hand to his mom to shake.

"So nice to meet you, dear, in spite of the circumstances," Sarah said. "Of course I blame his father," she continued. "The male decides the sex of the baby. After five boys I said *enough!*"

Lucy had returned to check on Molly, since the vet hadn't arrived yet, and chuckled at his mom's remark. Adam saw Carly Spencer's mouth turn up in a smile. She'd be even prettier if she smiled more often. Still, she didn't have much to be happy about, since her home had just gone up in flames.

"Ouch!" he yelped as Lucy reached over and prodded him.

"She's only trying to help, darling," his mother pointed out. "If you can't be more civil, you'll never find anyone to marry you."

"Sometimes your conversation defies logic, Mom," he muttered through the mask. He pulled it away from his face so she couldn't mistake his words. "And I'm not looking for a wife," he said, hoping she'd go away. And take the Carly woman with her.

"Oh, my God, you're gay!" his mom said, as if this was a revelation that explained everything—his unmarried state, his aversion to moving back to his hometown, possibly even the cause of global warming.

"Not that there's anything wrong with that, of course," she added quickly.

"I'm not gay."

"You've never had a relationship."

"Trust me, Mom, I've had relationships."

"With women?"

"*Of course with women!* Mom, seriously, you're acting weird."

"I just want to ensure the continuation of the O'Malley line."

"Last count, you had seven grandkids. The O'Malley line is safe."

"But…"

Adam forced himself to sit up. "Once and for all, Mom. *I am not gay!*"

Everything seemed to freeze—the chattering of by-standers, the whine of emergency vehicles, even the sound of water gushing from the fire hoses.

Heads swiveled in Adam's direction. His colleagues, several of whom had stood down now the blaze was under control, turned toward him and stared. Louella snorted.

The television crews zeroed in on a developing human interest story. The Carly woman shifted her kid to the other hip and smiled.

Adam groaned.

His mom looked as if she wanted to argue further. Adam lay back down, replaced the oxygen mask over his face and closed his eyes.

Moments later, he heard his mother huff and go off in search of someone else to pester.

"Your mom seems concerned about you."

"She's concerned about everyone. Unfortunately, she's *insanely* overprotective of me." He wanted to assure her he wasn't gay, but what was she to him? No one impor-tant. Just the mom of a kid he'd rescued. He'd never see her again after today. What did it matter what she thought about his sexuality? What did it matter what anyone thought? Even his mom.

"You're the youngest?"

He opened an eye. "How'd you guess?" He felt he had to at least try to be polite, since this woman had just lost her home. In reality, he didn't want to talk to anyone right now. Especially anyone of the female sex. Between his mom's nagging, this woman's nosiness, Lucy's brutal treatment, Molly the dog and Louella the pig slobbering on him, he'd had his fill of females for the day. What he really wanted was to take a long shower, have a beer and maybe watch a hockey game on TV with his dad. His dad rarely talked, never nagged. Mac O'Malley, patriarch of the O'Malley clan, was probably his best friend in the world. Pity Adam would never be able to talk about the night Rory Bennett died, even with Mac.

"Mothers have a special place in their hearts for the baby of the family."

Did this woman ever shut up? Adam wondered. He was so sick of being called the *baby* of the family.

"Ma'am?" Adam was thankful when his captain's voice intruded. He wanted to sleep instead of being surrounded by chattering people. Most of them women. "Your kids have all been cleared by the paramedics. You're good to go."

"Thank you. Thank you for everything," she said. Then her lip quivered.

Oh, no, here come the tears, Adam thought.

Sure enough, the woman started to cry.

"Hey, there," Lucy said, patting her back. "Your children are fine." She pulled out her cell. "Who can I call for you? Do you have family nearby or friends you can stay with?"

The woman shook her head and staggered away.

Adam had never seen anyone look so desolate in his life. And he'd seen a lot of sorrow during his years in this job.

"Oh, my goodness." His mom appeared out of nowhere and went to comfort the woman. She glared at Adam over her shoulder, as if he was the cause of her misery.

Adam strained to hear what they said to each other, then gave up. Lucy had given him the all clear, and Martin had released him from duty for the rest of his shift. It was time to head home and hit the shower. He sat up and glanced around. There were even more spectators than when he'd brought the dog down the ladder.

He could see his brother Matt conferring with the television crew. Matt was nodding his head. He turned in Adam's direction and waved. Then he smiled. Matt rarely smiled.

As a youngster, Adam had held out for praise and encouragement from his big brother. He'd come to learn that exuberance wasn't Matt's way. A wave and smile would be all the compliment Adam could expect.

He stood too quickly and stumbled, but was caught by Matt's strong arms before he hit the ground. "Hey, easy there, kid," he said. "Sit down for a bit."

Exhausted, Adam could only shake his head. "Need to get out of here. Take a shower."

Molly was still lying on her back playing dead—except her tail was wagging. Matt bent down and rubbed her tummy. She rewarded him with a squirm of pleasure.

"The television people want to interview you." Matt indicated the crew he'd been speaking to behind the police cordon.

"What for?" Adam looked away from their prying cameras. "I was just doing my job."

He felt Matt's hand on his shoulder and welcomed its warmth. "You're a hero, little brother."

He hated that word. He was no hero. "Like I said, I was just doing my job. Do you do interviews every time you arrest some bad guy?"

"You saved the life of a child and a dog. You know how this town loves dogs."

"Then tell 'em to donate generously to the pound." Adam was fed up with talking. "Where's your vehicle?" he asked. "Can you drive me home?"

Matt crossed his arms in a gesture that said he wasn't pleased. "Since you live at home, why don't you have Mom take you?"

"Because I want peace and quiet, not Mom alternating between singing my praises and getting hysterical about how risky my job is."

"Mom is never hysterical."

"You didn't see her earlier."

"Darling!"

"Speak of the devil," Adam muttered as their mother returned.

"Could you drive Adam home?" she said to Matt. "Carly and her children don't have anyone to stay with, so I've offered them the apartment over the stables for as long as they need it. Molly's coming, too."

What am I? Chopped liver? Adam felt like asking. Instead, he said, "In case you've forgotten, Mom, *I'm* living in the apartment over the stables."

"Yes, I'm aware of that, darling, but I'm moving you into the house so Carly and her little brood can have some privacy. You don't mind, do you?" Without waiting for his answer, she turned away and directed the Carly woman and her children toward her SUV.

Adam stared after her. "Is this the same person who,

last week when I returned home, practically kissed the ground I walked on?"

"The very same," Matt said. "You know Mom can't resist a waif, and now she's got five of them to care for. Correction—six." Matt indicated Molly being lifted from her stretcher by one of the firefighters and carried to his mom's vehicle.

"Can I stay at your place?" Adam begged. Matt and his wife, Beth, lived in a large home their brother Jack had built them in a picturesque valley outside town. Adam would love to live in that same valley one day. Someday. After he'd confronted his demons.

"Sure. I did tell you Sarah's teething, didn't I?"

"No, you didn't. Now that you mention it, maybe I *would* be better off at home," Adam said, and followed Matt to his vehicle. Although where he'd sleep, Adam had no idea, since one of his three nieces was occupying his old bedroom.

As it turned out, his tomboy of a niece Daisy was only too happy to give up her room to her "hero" uncle. So Adam slept among her animal posters and woke up during the night with a lump under the mattress that turned out to be a stirrup. He pulled it out, tossed it on the floor, coughed up more black goop and went back to sleep.

Chapter Two

Awakened the next morning by pandemonium from the kitchen, Adam recognized the deep pitch of several of his brothers' voices and an occasional "Shh!" from his mom.

He stumbled out of bed, washed his face but didn't bother shaving and went downstairs, hungry enough to eat one of their prize black Angus steers all by himself. He'd missed dinner since he'd taken the much-wanted shower and fallen into bed, exhausted, and slept through the night.

Sunday mornings, the family usually gathered at Two Elk Ranch for breakfast. However, today was Saturday, Adam noted as he strode into the kitchen, a huge room that accommodated the family dining table. Today it was packed to overflowing with all his brothers.

"Here he is!" Celeste, his youngest niece, cried and ran to him, her arms outstretched.

Adam bent to lift Celeste the way he'd done a hundred times before, but as he did, a muscle twitched with pain. He grunted and nearly dropped her.

His reaction had most of the occupants of the kitchen rushing forward to help him. He held out a hand to restrain them and ruffled Celeste's hair. "Next time, kiddo," he said. "I must've put out something in my back."

He rubbed at the spot, but couldn't quite reach it.

"Then it's lucky Carly is a massage therapist," his brother Will said. He came around the table to clap Adam on the back, making him wince. "And in case I didn't say it yesterday, well done, little brother. Anyone who saves a dog is good people in my book."

Speaking of the dog, he wondered where she was. Adam tried not to groan as Will slapped him again.

"You should have Carly look at that," his mom said.

"I'd be happy to."

Adam glanced around and found the woman with too many children, with the littlest one perched on her hip. She seemed slightly less vulnerable than she had the last time he'd seen her. The toddler's face was covered with goo that might or might not have been oatmeal. He smiled and waved at Adam. Adam forced himself to smile back. He smiled at the mom, too—but not an overly friendly smile, since she and her kids were responsible for getting him booted out of the apartment above the stables.

He wished he could disappear. He wasn't comfortable with crowds, even if he *was* related to most of the people there. How he missed the seclusion of that apartment.

Then his eyes fell on the newspaper spread across the table and his stomach lurched. The headline, Hometown Hero, glared up at Adam, along with a photo of him carrying the child out of the burning apartment building. A smaller one showed him and Molly lying on their stretchers side by side. Unfortunately, it also featured Louella kissing him. The caption beneath read *Mayor's Pet Pig Thanks Heroic Firefighter Adam O'Malley.*

Adam hated seeing the word *hero* associated with his name. He was no hero. Heroes didn't let their friend take the rap for a fatal car accident.

His dad came forward and clapped him on the back. Like his two oldest sons, Luke and Matt, Mac O'Malley was a man of few words. Adam figured his mom more than made up for it. He didn't expect his dad to say anything, so when Adam saw tears brimming in his eyes, he nodded and let his dad pass by him and leave the kitchen.

His brother Jack came over and was about to clap him on the back, too, but Adam held up his hand and Jack dropped his. "Sore, eh, buddy?" Jack asked, and Adam nodded.

"I'm so proud of you," Jack said. Then tears welled in his eyes, as well.

Oh, jeez, this was what he didn't need, an outpouring of emotion from the O'Malley men. Although he and Jack were separated in age by only eleven months, they were pretty much opposite in temperament. Jack wore his heart on his sleeve; Adam wasn't sure if he even had a heart.

Coming back to town had been a bad idea. He shouldn't have accepted that one-month posting to Spruce Lake to cover an absence in the department. He should've gone somewhere else in Colorado. *Anywhere* else! But his mom had pressured him to take the posting, saying he was missing out on seeing his nieces and nephews growing up.

Adam had enough guilt to deal with, so he'd agreed to the job, telling himself it was only for a month. He could survive a month without having to get too close to anyone or having to care too much. And then he could return to Boulder, where no one knew anything about his past and no one ever pried into his private business.

"Thank you for saving Molly, mister."

Adam looked down into the pale blue eyes of the Carly woman's daughter. Sheesh! Her eyes were brimming, too.

He patted her on the head. "You're welcome, kid." And then to deflect the gratitude of the rest of the children who were moving in his direction, he asked, "So where's Molly?"

"She's right here, Uncle Adam." He heard Luke's middle daughter Daisy's voice from somewhere behind the crowd in the kitchen. He walked toward it and found her seated on the floor, the dog's head in her lap. Daisy had always had a way with animals.

As much as it was possible for a basset to look anything but deeply saddened by life, the dog had an expression of bliss on her face as Daisy stroked her ears.

Molly was lying on a blanket. A blanket Adam recognized from his childhood. A blanket he was very fond of.

"That's *my* blanket," he couldn't help saying, and turned accusingly to his mother.

She flapped the spatula at him and said, "You haven't used that in years. So I've given it to Molly. She needs it more than you."

"I might have *wanted* to use it," he muttered. It was the principle of the thing. He mightn't have used the blanket for more than twenty years, but it was a well-worn and much-loved childhood companion, and for some stupid reason he felt a sense of possessiveness about it. It sure as hell didn't deserve to be used as a *dog* blanket.

"It's Molly's now," Daisy piped up.

His oldest brother, Luke, who ran the family ranch, pressed him down into one of the vacated chairs at the table that occupied the huge country-style kitchen. The table easily sat ten, twelve at a pinch, and today people were rotating chairs as they finished breakfast and made way for the next shift.

He took his seat—beside Carly—and studied the occupants of the kitchen. Although heavily pregnant, Luke's wife, Megan, was helping his mom prepare and serve. Luke's oldest daughter, Sasha, was talking to Will's stepson, Nick, while Celeste, Luke's youngest, was chatting animatedly with the little girl who'd thanked him before. The two boys who belonged to Carly were bolting down second helpings of oatmeal like they hadn't been fed in a week. Maybe they hadn't, Adam decided. Their apartment wasn't exactly in the town's high-rent district.

And where was their father? he wanted to ask, not for the first time. Shouldn't *he* be taking care of his family?

"Where's your husband?" Adam blurted, before he could stop himself.

Silence descended on the kitchen and Adam wished the floor would open up.

She looked back at him with a frankness that was daunting and said, "He's dead."

CARLY SPENCER TOOK GRIM satisfaction in watching Adam O'Malley's discomfort as he swallowed her answer and half hoped he'd choke on it. She'd already told Adam's family that her husband, Michael, was a firefighter who'd perished in a warehouse fire in San Diego. She'd been seven months pregnant with Charlie at the time.

And now she felt bad about her bald statement. She, of all people, having been married to a firefighter, should've been more circumspect. But something perverse had made her answer his question as rudely as it had been asked.

What was it with this guy? He had the nicest, most welcoming family, but he was so emotionally distant, it was almost scary.

He'd done the bravest thing yesterday, not only rescuing her son Charlie but defying his battalion chief's orders and saving Molly. Yet when she'd tried to thank him, he'd been so offhand it bordered on arrogant.

She'd wanted to call him on his behavior, but there

was something in Adam O'Malley's dark brown eyes that spoke of a hurt far greater than Carly suspected he ever revealed to others. So instead of challenging him further, she asked, "Would you like some bacon?" and passed the plate to him without waiting for his answer.

His mother came up behind him and scooped scrambled eggs onto his plate, kissing the top of his head as she did.

Carly didn't miss the deep blush beneath his tan. That was interesting, the relationship between him and his mom. She got the feeling Sarah irritated him at times. Like now. She was bent over him from behind, hugging him.

"Mom. *Please?*" he murmured.

"I'm just so happy to have you home. And alive," his mom said, and kissed the top of his head again before releasing him. The guy was clearly embarrassed by his mother's display of affection. Sarah, however, seemed to revel in exasperating—if that was the right word—her youngest son, as if she was deliberately trying to provoke a reaction.

She returned with the coffeepot and poured Adam a cup, then went to put cream in it. He took the jug from her hand and murmured, "I can do it myself, Mom."

"Of course you can, darling," she said, totally unfazed, "but you're a hero, and I intend to make you feel like one."

Carly noticed that her own sons, sitting across the table from them, were transfixed by the exchange. To diffuse their interest, she said, "I don't believe you've been properly introduced to my children. The one who caused you so much trouble yesterday is Alex and the one beside him who's eating as if he hasn't been fed in a week is Jake. My daughter is Madeleine. And this little guy," she said, indicating her youngest, sitting on her lap, "is Charlie."

Charlie, far from being grateful to his savior, chose that moment to flick a spoonful of oatmeal at Adam. Then he laughed.

TO HIS CREDIT, ADAM didn't leap from his seat or demand an apology. Instead, he wiped the oatmeal from his cheek with his finger, then wiped his finger on his napkin. "It's gratifying to be reminded of what the public thinks of *we who serve them*," he said, and dug into his eggs.

Will patted him gently on the back. "That's the spirit, buddy. Nothing like some creative criticism to bring you back to earth. Can't have you walking around the ranch with a head bigger than a black Angus bull."

Luke laughed from where he stood beside the kitchen range and raised his coffee mug in agreement.

Carly liked the oldest of the O'Malley brothers. Hey, she liked them all. She was trying to like Adam, too, but he wasn't exactly making it easy for her. *What's his problem?* she wondered.

He was eating in silence. Probably trying to ignore her. Well, that was fine because she didn't want to make conversation with him, either.

She sipped her coffee, savoring the richness of the blend—a far cry from the budget brand she usually drank. Various conversations flowed around the kitchen and she caught snippets of them and smiled. Maddy and Celeste seemed to have hit it off. They were both in first grade but in different classes and hadn't met each other before. Carly liked Celeste. She was an angelic-looking child with a sweet temperament and outgoing personality. Maddy was more withdrawn, but Celeste seemed to have struck a chord with her as they shared a love of drawing. The pair were presently giggling over pictures they'd drawn of Adam.

Carly wanted to see how he'd react to them and asked, "What have you got there, Maddy?"

Her daughter held up the picture. She'd given Adam curly, dark brown hair and a smiley face. Carly glanced at Adam. His hair was indeed dark brown, but cut so short, it was hard to determine if there was any curl in it.

Then Celeste held up her picture. She'd given Adam even curlier and longer hair. The child apparently knew her uncle well enough to have done that. However, instead of a smiley face, Adam's expression was angry.

"Why did you draw your uncle looking so annoyed?" she asked Celeste.

"He's not. He's thinking," the child corrected her. "He frowns when he thinks. Like he is now." Celeste indicated her uncle with a flick of her head, bit into a bagel her father had smeared with cream cheese and honey and went back to her drawing.

An odd combination, Carly thought as Celeste wolfed it down. She turned to Adam. Sure enough, he was frowning. But he was miles away and not part of the conversation, nor had he seemed to notice the girls' drawings of him.

"A penny for them," she ventured, wanting to make friends with the man who'd saved her son's life.

"What?" he said, coming out of his reverie.

"You were deep in thought," she said. "If your back is bothering you, I'd be happy to give you a massage. It's the least I can do."

He put down his coffee cup and looked at her. "Thank you, but no." He stood. "I have to be going. There'll be a disciplinary meeting because I ignored my chief's orders," he said to the room's occupants.

"And saved Molly," Carly finished for him, knowing he'd never say the words himself. "I hope you don't get into too much trouble. If there's anything I can say to whoever you have to answer to, I will. I'll testify that Alex would have run into that building to get her if you hadn't."

"I doubt a kid would be any match for a firefighter," he said, his voice sardonic, then abruptly left the kitchen.

The rest of the adults had taken their seats at the table and were looking at her.

"I…I'm sorry, I don't know what I said to make him leave like that."

Sarah leaned over and touched her hand. "Don't pay any attention to him, dear."

She didn't go on to excuse his behavior or explain it, so Carly busied herself with clearing the table. "I wanted to thank you again…for welcoming my children and me into your home." Carly could feel her voice breaking, but she continued, hoping to find the strength she needed.

She could do it. She'd survived her husband, Michael's, accidental death. She'd survived this past year and a half without her parents' support or knowledge of how bad things were for her financially.

Her dad had suffered a stroke early last year and Carly had no intention of burdening him or her mother with her latest woes. They had enough to deal with.

She could survive the aftermath of this fire and start fresh. Just like she had before.

She'd used Michael's insurance money to pay off their house in San Diego. And to pay off his credit card debts, which had been considerable. His fascination with the latest toys—from snowmobiles to Jet Skis, Windsurfers to water skis—had been a bone of contention in their marriage. Carly hadn't realized how tangled their finances were until she opened the bills addressed to Michael after his death.

Once she'd paid off the mortgage, she'd felt more secure, knowing that no matter what, her children would always have a roof over their heads. But less than a year after doing that, Carly had wanted to get out of San Diego. Not so much to escape the memories but to escape the unwanted attentions of Michael's best friend and fellow firefighter, Jerry Ryan.

Jerry had been a wonderful support after Michael's death, but his behavior had become too familiar, bordering on obsessive, and Carly had felt trapped. She'd decided to move away from San Diego, the memories—and Jerry.

She'd rented out her home, effective January 1, intending to live off the rent and her work as a massage therapist.

Neither her parents nor Jerry were happy with her decision to move out of the state, but Carly remained resolute.

Offered a job at a new spa hotel opening in Denver, she'd accepted. She and the children had spent Christmas with her parents, then moved to the Mile High City a week before the hotel was slated to open in the new year. She'd enrolled her children in school and paid the security deposit to rent an apartment near work. But the day before opening, the hotel was firebombed. Fortunately, nobody had died, and both police and press speculated that organized crime had been responsible.

To Carly's immense gratitude, her new landlord had been compassionate about her situation and come up with a solution. He owned an apartment building in the mountain town of Spruce Lake. In the summer it would be demolished and a new complex built in its place, but in the meantime, he had a vacancy available. If she could find herself a job in Spruce Lake, the apartment was hers. He assured her he could easily fill the vacancy in the Denver apartment she'd be leaving.

Carly had jumped at the opportunity, knowing that resort towns were often in need of massage therapists. She had her own massage table and could supplement her income by offering massages to people in the privacy of their homes.

Nearly two months had passed since that fateful day in Denver. Carly hadn't told her parents about the firebombing and her move to Spruce Lake; she hadn't wanted to worry them. Instead, she'd been upbeat in her emails and Skype calls.

And there was another reason she hadn't wanted to come clean about her move. She knew Jerry kept in touch with her folks. She didn't want him to learn where she was.

Her children had settled into Spruce Lake Elementary and were loving it. Carly liked the warmth of the community and was gradually building a client base of locals and tourists. Charlie went to daycare a couple of days a week while Carly worked. She also did a few shifts at the local spa. Finding a reliable after-school sitter for the children on the days she had to work hadn't been too difficult—until yesterday.

If she could have replayed yesterday, she'd never have left her children with a sitter she didn't know. And if Sarah O'Malley hadn't come to their rescue, Carly had no idea what she could've done. The O'Malleys were the kindest, most giving people she'd ever met.

But the raw anger, the fear and desperation she'd experienced when she realized Charlie was missing still ate at her.

"You've been so…generous…and we don't…" she started to say, but then the floodgates opened. The tears she'd held so tightly in check after the fire, the emotions she'd suppressed all through the endless night, flowed.

Conscious that she was making a complete fool of herself, Carly blubbered an apology. But warm arms enveloped her and Carly turned to cry on the offered shoulder, finding it was Mac who'd silently reentered the kitchen.

"There, there," she heard Sarah say. "Let it all out, dear. You've been holding it in, being brave for too long."

Sarah was right; she *had* been holding it in, putting on a brave face for her kids, and now that they'd left the room, she'd fallen apart.

"I'm sorry," she said to Mac, lifting her head and seeing the huge damp patch on his shirt. A wad of tissues got shoved into her hand and she tried to staunch her running nose and wipe at her eyes. Mac rubbed her back in soothing circles and said, "You lean on me all you want, Carly."

Carly sobbed at the warmth and compassion in his voice and wished her father could be there for her.

When she'd composed herself a little, she looked up into Mac's eyes and in a vulnerable moment admitted she wished her father was there. And then she wished she could take back her words, because they were too revealing. It was too much to admit to these people who until last night were strangers.

Megan hugged Mac as well, and said, "I wish I'd had a dad like Mac. I'm so glad I married Luke."

Grateful for Megan's lifeline, Carly wondered what Megan's family history had been for her to make a remark like that.

"Let's not overdo it!" When Mac finally managed to struggle out of their embrace, he was blushing. Molly got up from her blanket and came over to nudge his leg, whimpering as if in agreement. "Women!" he muttered good-naturedly, grabbed his hat and took off out the back door.

Sarah chuckled and said, "I think the estrogen overload was getting to him."

Megan smiled, dabbing at her eyes. "He needs to get used to it. He has a wife, three daughters-in-law and five granddaughters."

That broke the remaining tension in the room and the rest of the occupants laughed.

"Women!" This came from Luke and Megan's son, Cody, whom Carly had learned was the result of a holiday romance Luke and Megan had had sixteen years earlier. They'd only recently been reunited and still acted like newlyweds. Sasha, Daisy and Celeste were by Luke's ex-wife—the mention of whom had caused Sarah's lips to purse and Luke to change the subject.

Carly hadn't quite got all the family relationships sorted out, but they were gradually falling into place.

Like his grandfather, Cody grabbed his hat and headed out the back door.

"I agree with them," Luke said. "There are way too many women around here." He kissed his wife and removed his hat from the peg near the back door, then followed his father and son out to start work.

"I'd better check in with the office," Matt said, standing.

Jack glanced at his watch. "And I have an appointment with Frank Farquar. Seems the mayor wants me to build a stronger porch swing for Louella."

"Louella?" Carly asked.

"The mayor's pet pig," Will explained. "She was hanging around with me at the fire. I'll introduce you sometime."

The brothers said their goodbyes, leaving Carly and Sarah alone in the kitchen. Carly stood, ready to clean up, but Sarah indicated she should sit.

She took a seat opposite Carly, poured more coffee and said, "Now, tell me, dear, how I can help?"

"You've done so much for us already. I don't know what we would've done without you." Sarah had produced clothes and pajamas for her children last night, since they'd had only the clothes they were standing in. Carly appreciated how Sarah did everything without fuss, saving her children from any further distress. If it had been her own mother in similar circumstances, it would've felt as if Carly was swept up in a tornado. Carly's mom thrived on drama. It was one of the reasons she hadn't turned to them after Michael's death. And now that her dad was ill, there was no way Carly would even think of adding to his problems.

"Dear, I know you lost everything in that fire. I'm pretty sure the only possession you have left is your vehicle, and that got so much water damage parked where it was, it'll take a while to get fixed."

Carly nodded. She needed her minivan for work. Not that she had a job anymore since her mobile massage table was destroyed in the fire. She wished she'd had it in her van, but she'd left it upstairs because Mrs. Polinski had booked a massage after Carly's appointments at the spa. And now she'd inherited the Polinskis' dog.

Yesterday as they were loaded into the ambulance, Mrs. Polinski had asked Carly to look after Molly while they were in the hospital, but as of this morning, Molly was homeless. When Carly had called the hospital to find out how they were doing, she'd been put through to Mrs. Polinski, who'd been very upset that they'd be moving back east with their son and daughter-in-law. Apparently, their son's wife didn't want Molly coming with them. The old lady was understandably upset about Molly, and Carly promised to see what she could do. Unfortunately, Mrs. Polinski had misunderstood and thought Carly was adopting the dog.

So now it looked as if Molly belonged to her. Could her life get any more complicated? Oh, yeah, it could. Molly was due to be spayed the week after next and she'd just bet that hadn't been prepaid!

Although Carly had no possessions left in Spruce Lake, at least she had her precious children. And that was all that mattered. From what she'd been able to glean talking to the babysitter afterward, there'd been a tremendous explosion that shook the building, followed shortly after by one of the other residents screaming, "Fire!" Then all hell had broken loose.

Tiffany had grabbed the three oldest children and fled down the stairs, just as Carly had pulled up outside the building. When Carly had asked her where Charlie was, she admitted she'd forgotten all about him. Carly forced the memory of that horrible moment out of her mind and told herself, *Charlie is fine. Your children are all fine. You will get through this.*

"I have nothing left," Carly said. "I hadn't gotten around to taking out insurance on our possessions." Meager as they were, she added silently.

"I feel so overwhelmed! I don't know how I'm going to get my business going again." She fought the tears that threatened. Feeling sorry for herself wouldn't get her anywhere. She needed to find some money to buy a new massage table and start earning again. She'd resented Michael for spending their savings on frivolous toys she'd had to sell for a tenth of their value when he'd died. And now she'd been just as reckless by not insuring their possessions.

"So you don't have any savings?" Sarah asked.

Carly took a deep breath. She'd already told Sarah about her dad's stroke and how she didn't want to burden her parents.

"There've been too many bills to pay lately, what with moving costs, getting established in the apartment, paying for utilities—it all costs money."

Afraid the older woman would see her as a loser for not having saved anything, she quickly added, "But I have a home in San Diego. It's rented out. When my husband died I used the insurance money to pay off the mortgage and our credit card debts. Then…" Carly didn't want to go into why she'd decided to leave San Diego, didn't want to talk about Jerry Ryan getting too possessive of her. She'd tried letting him down nicely, but it had become very uncomfortable. In the end she'd used the excuse that she needed to get out of San Diego, to start her life anew.

"Unfortunately, the global financial crisis meant I couldn't sell the house for anything near what we paid for it. So I decided to rent it out and relocate. The rent helps with my expenses for now, but there's not much left over once all the bills are paid. In a few years, when the real estate market's recovered, I'll sell it and buy something here—if I can afford to."

Sarah's smile lit up the room. "So you like Spruce Lake? In spite of the fire?"

"I love it. My children are happy at school, even though we've been here such a short time. And Spruce Lake is delightful. It has everything I could ask for."

"I'm so glad you like our little town. I fell in love with it, too, on my first visit with Mac."

"I'd like to get established in my own business here,

build up a good client base, but without a massage table, I'm going to have to cancel the appointments I had booked for next week." Carly brushed her hair back and said, "Well, I guess I'd better get cleaned up and make an appointment with the bank manager. Plead with him to lend me enough to buy a new one so I can get started again."

"That's the spirit!" Sarah said, lifting Carly's own spirits immensely. "I like the way you think, Carly."

"I don't know how to thank you. You've done so much for me. You're a godsend," Carly said. "In fact, last night I woke up and wondered if I was dreaming. Not about the fire, but about how kind you were. How safe you made me feel."

Sarah rewarded her with another smile. "You're welcome, dear. Now, you go see if you can get an appointment today. I'll clean up here."

"Oh, no, you don't! Look at this place! It's a disaster."

Sarah glanced around. "True," she agreed. "But I like it that way. Makes me feel needed. You run along." She made shooing motions. "I'll have the girls help me clean up. You don't mind if I rope Maddy in, do you? That's how they earn their allowance."

"What a good idea. I'd get the boys to help, too, but they seem to have taken off to watch Luke with the horses." She could see her boys through the kitchen window, sitting on the corral fence as Luke worked with a horse.

"They'll get their turn," Sarah assured her. She took Charlie from Carly's arms and sat him in a high chair, then gave him a piece of toast. "He'll be fine here with me. And if you have to go into town this morning, I'll watch the children."

Carly was about to say "thank you" yet again when Sarah held up her hand. "I know. I know," she said.

"Carly, it's my pleasure. I love having this house full of people. Now, off you go."

CARLY WENT INTO THE living room, looked up her bank's number and called using the house phone. She'd been in such a panic that she'd left her cell phone in her minivan when she'd leaped out. It was too water damaged to ever work again.

Five minutes later, Carly's hopes had been completely dashed. After she explained the situation to her bank manager, he'd refused her a loan. Since she hadn't applied for a credit card, not wanting to be hit with high interest rates if she was late with payments and with the memory of the debt Michael had built up so easily, Carly only had a debit card. But there was barely enough in her account to buy a pair of warm winter boots for herself to replace those she'd lost in the fire. She wore clean white tennis shoes to her spa appointments, wanting to look professional and be comfortable. But tennis shoes were useless for walking in snow and ice, and since it was winter, she'd be doing a lot of that.

Carly sat on the sofa, bit her lip and forced herself not to cry. How many more things could go wrong with her life? As if sensing her melancholy, Molly waddled into the room and curled up on Carly's feet. Carly reached down to rub the dog's ears. "Poor girl, you're missing your owners, aren't you?" she asked, then jumped as a wad of money was thrust under her nose.

She stared at it, bewildered.

"Take it," Adam said gruffly.

"I…I can't do that."

"Yeah. You can. I heard your half of the conversation. You need it more than I do."

Carly shook her head and glanced up at Adam. "Thank

you, but no. I'll find some way to get my business up and running again without accepting charity."

"Then give me a massage and I'll pay for it."

"I don't have a table," she pointed out.

He shrugged and proffered the money again. "So go buy a table with this and then pay me back with a massage."

Carly couldn't help smiling at his logic. "You're talking a lot of massages!"

"I've got a feeling I'll need them after I've met with my supervisors today."

Remembering the conversation before Adam had come downstairs this morning—his family was concerned about disciplinary action for disobeying his battalion chief's orders—she said, "I...I hope it goes well for you, Adam. What you did was nothing short of heroic." Her eyes filled with tears and she dashed them away. "I'm sorry I'm being so emotional. I'm not usually this weepy, but when I think of what might've happened to Charlie if you hadn't found him. And Molly, she's such a sweet dog...I...can't...help...it."

"Yeah. Well," he said, scratched Molly's head and left the room.

His sudden departure shocked Carly so much that she stopped crying. *Must get more control of emotions!* she told herself, and looked up. Adam had left the wad of notes on the coffee table.

She took them to the kitchen.

Sarah heard her entering, turned around and smiled. "How'd it go?" she asked.

"I, ah," Carly faltered, and held out the notes to Sarah.

"Goodness! That was quick," the older woman quipped. "Did he send you that through the phone line?" she asked with a grin.

"Quite the contrary. My *ex*–bank manager doesn't want anything to do with me. Adam gave me this, but I can't accept it."

Sarah's eyebrows rose. "And you told him so?"

"Of course."

"And?"

"He said I can work off the debt with massages."

"Who said that?" Megan asked, coming into the kitchen.

"Carly's bank manager won't let her have a loan to get her business up and running again, so Adam's given her an advance payment for services to be rendered. That way she can buy a massage table," Sarah explained. She rubbed her shoulders. "Hmm. I think I need to prepurchase a ten-pack of massages. Do you do discounts for friends?" she asked with a twinkle in her eye.

"You know perfectly well I wouldn't consider charging you," Carly said, and wagged her finger at Sarah.

"Then you can charge me," Megan said. "I've heard prenatal massages are wonderful for expectant moms."

"They are," Carly agreed. "But I couldn't charge you, either! You've already given me half your wardrobe," she said, referring to Megan's generous offer of clothes.

"I won't be able to fit into them for a while yet, so you're welcome." Megan brushed off her concerns. "Now, when can I book my first massage?"

"As soon as I can get a table," Carly said, shaking the money at her.

"Can you buy one locally?" Sarah asked. "If not, we could make a run down to Denver." She glanced at Megan. "After all, I have a nursery to furnish for my next grandchild, and although I like to buy locally, there are a few things I can't get up here."

"True!" Megan said, her face lighting up. "I feel a shopping trip coming on!"

Carly wished she could join in with their enthusiasm, but she simply didn't have the funds. She hadn't counted the money Adam had given her, but there couldn't be enough for a massage table, could there?

"You look worried," Sarah said. "If you can't buy a table around here, I really did mean we could take a trip to Denver."

Carly forced a smile into her voice and said, "Let me make a few calls, and if I can't buy one here today, I'll take you up on that."

Megan pulled out her cell and said, "You know, I think the other women in my prenatal class would love to sign up for some treatments with you."

"So would the ladies in my quilting group," Sarah chimed in. She, too, pulled out her cell. "Let's all meet back here in half an hour and see what we've come up with."

Chapter Three

Exactly thirty minutes later, they met back in the living room. Sarah produced a list of at least a dozen names. "And more to come," she promised. Megan had an equally long list.

"Then that settles it," Carly said. "The trip to Denver is on, if you're still offering, because I can buy a massage table direct from the wholesaler."

Sarah rubbed her hands together. "I'll make sandwiches for the men's lunch. If you like, Carly, we can leave the boys here under Luke's watchful eye. I checked on them before, and he and one of the hands are teaching them to ride. I don't think you'll be able to drag them away to go shopping."

When Carly nodded, Sarah went on. "Now, we'll take Charlie and the two little girls. Daisy will want to stay here with her father. Sasha may or may not want to come with us."

"Come where?" Sasha asked as she breezed into the room.

"Shopping in Denver," her grandmother replied.

The magic word effectively stopped the teen in her tracks. "I'll be ready in five," she said, and ran back upstairs to her room.

"I'll let the guys know they're fending for themselves

until we get back," Megan said as she pulled on a warm jacket and hurried out the back door.

"And I'll help make sandwiches," Carly said, her earlier enthusiasm returning.

CARLY DIDN'T THINK IT was possible to go from feeling so completely desolate and alone to being on such a high in less than twenty-four hours.

In the past day, she'd gone from having nothing to having a new start in life, two new and already very dear friends and a measure of happiness that had been missing even before the dreadful fire that had claimed her husband's life.

Adam's money had purchased a better and sturdier massage table than she'd had before. There was even a little left over so she'd treated Megan and Sarah to coffee at a bookstore and the children to thick shakes.

They'd returned to Two Elk Ranch in high spirits, loaded down with maternity clothes for Megan, items for the nursery and new clothes for the girls and for Carly's two boys.

Sasha dashed upstairs to change into one of her new outfits, accompanied by Maddy and Celeste. Sarah disappeared into her wing of the house to find Mac, and Megan went in search of Luke to have him unpack the car, leaving Carly alone in the living room.

Only she wasn't alone for long, because Adam stalked through the room muttering something about screaming girls.

He stopped short when he realized he wasn't alone.

"Was your trip a success?" he asked shortly, as if he didn't care one way or the other.

Carly decided not to let it bother her. "Yes, it was. Thanks to you. And how did your...meeting go today?"

Carly didn't miss the grimace before he got his emotions under control. "Not so good. I have to appear before a disciplinary board on Monday."

"I'm sorry. You deserve better treatment than that," Carly said, meaning it.

He shrugged. "Goes with the territory. I was about to get myself a beer to drown my sorrows. Can I get anything for you...or the kid?" he asked, indicating Charlie, nestled on her hip.

"His name is Charlie," she said, determined not to ignore Adam's "pretending he didn't care about anything" act.

"Charlie, then," he said, and without waiting for her answer, went into the kitchen.

Carly followed him and found him with his head buried in the fridge. "Want a beer?" he asked from the depths of it.

"A soda would be absolutely marvelous. Thank you," she said flippantly, then chided herself for her sarcasm. The man might be a Neanderthal, but he'd saved her son's life. She needed to overlook his personality defects and be kind and understanding.

"Kind and understanding, Carly," she muttered under her breath.

"You say something?" he asked, holding up several varieties of soda.

She selected one and opened it. "Nothing important," she said, noticing how he winced as he took a seat at the table. "Why don't we set up my new table and get started on those therapeutic massages I owe you?" she suggested.

He glanced up at her, eyes narrowed. "Are you really a *qualified* massage therapist?"

"What's that supposed to mean?" she snapped, at the end of her patience.

He shrugged again, annoying her even more. The guy did a lot of shrugging and she suspected it was his way of pretending nothing mattered.

Carly took a seat across from him and slammed her soda down on the table. She experienced a small sense of satisfaction when he jumped. "I asked you a question," she said. "I don't accept shrugging as an answer and I'm sure your mother never did, either."

His dark eyes bored into hers but she refused to back down. He didn't like being challenged? Well, neither did she!

"When Will said you were a massage therapist, I envisioned you working in one of those massage parlors."

Carly could feel her blood beginning to boil. She'd suspected that was what he'd been hinting at, but something perverse made her want to hear him admit it.

"Do I *look* as though I work in a massage parlor?" she demanded.

"Wouldn't know. Never been in one."

Carly released a breath. "That makes two of us. For your information, I went to the American Institute of Massage Therapy and am qualified to give both therapeutic and sports massages. And I'll accept your abject apology for being such a jerk…on one condition."

"And that is?"

"That you help me unpack my new massage table from the car and specify where you'd like me to give you your first treatment."

A few interesting images of places Adam would like Carly to give him a massage came to mind. Most of them were X-rated, so he quashed that thought, resisting the urge to shrug—Carly was right; he did it too often. He got up and said, "Lead the way."

He watched as she stood and hoisted the kid onto her hip. "Why do you always carry him around?" he asked. "Can't he walk?" He regretted the belligerence of his tone the moment the words were out of his mouth. As he half expected, Carly managed to floor him with her answer.

"As a matter of fact, he can. However, since I nearly lost him in the fire yesterday, I'm reluctant to let him out of my grasp. If you don't mind me massaging you one-handed, that would be great, because I don't want to put him down. For anything."

"Fair enough," Adam said, knowing she was baiting him. "Maybe we'd better postpone that massage until he's asleep. In a bed. Or does he sleep on your hip, too?"

He could see her muttering something under her breath, but couldn't quite hear it.

"Funny," she finally said, and threw him an exaggerated grin, which made Adam feel like a complete heel for prodding her.

Carly opened the fridge and got out some cheese slices and bread. She prepared a sandwich with one hand, then balanced the kid on the countertop as she cut the sandwich in two. She gave one half to the child, and chose a banana from the fruit bowl. Lifting Charlie onto her hip again, she said, "Let's go."

Adam found himself obediently following her through the living room and out the front door toward the car. Dusk had descended while they were inside bickering—no, that wasn't the right word. Was there such a word as *repartee-ing?* He didn't know, but it sounded…friendlier.

She opened the rear door of his mom's SUV and was about to reach inside.

"Let me get that," he said, moving around Carly.

He enjoyed brushing against her, and saw her swallow before she stepped aside to allow him access to the truck.

He took out a box that looked much too small to be a massage table. "This is it?" he asked.

"Yes," she said in a reasonable voice. "It's a *portable* massage table, remember?" She turned toward the stables. "I also bought some lattes and shakes for the shopping party with the change. I hope you don't mind."

Adam could hear the mild sarcasm in her tone and ignored it. "Where are we going?" he asked.

She stopped in her tracks and he nearly barreled into her. "To the stables. I would've thought that was obvious."

"Why not the house?"

"Because Charlie is about ready for bed. His own bed. And the house will be much too noisy for you to be able to relax properly." She spoke slowly and clearly as if he were a little slow. "And one of the requirements of a good massage is to offer a zone of peace for the client."

"You sound like you're reciting that from a book."

"I am," she said, and turned back toward the stables.

As it turned out, Charlie needed a bath before bed. He'd finished the other half of his sandwich on the walk to the stables, then made a mess of eating the banana, and since there wasn't a bathtub in the apartment over the stables—*his* apartment over the stables, Adam noted, still feeling proprietary about it—Carly filled the deep kitchen sink with water and plopped Charlie into it.

Adam watched as she bathed her son. The pair seemed wrapped within a cocoon, safe together, mother humming and talking soothingly to her child.

He'd once felt safe like that, too. But years ago, something bad had happened, something he'd caused and never owned up to. Being back home was causing that memory, and the self-loathing that went with it, to resurface. He worked on pushing the thoughts away, taking deep breaths, then exhaling.

"Are you all right?" she asked, snapping him out of it. "I hope you're not suffering any aftereffects of the smoke inhalation."

Adam almost hated the concern he could hear in her voice. She sounded as if she cared. He didn't want people to care about him. Because that meant *he'd* have to care about *them*. He'd survived the past fifteen years by trying not to care.

She lifted Charlie from the sink and placed him on a towel on the counter and dried him off. "Nearly done, my little man," she cooed to the kid, then carried him to the sofa bed. "Just as well you're not too fussy yet. Otherwise, you wouldn't want to be wearing these Barbie pajamas. They used to be Celeste's," she told him as she diapered and dressed her son.

Carly tucked Charlie beneath the covers and kissed his cheek. He grabbed a rag doll, stuck it under his arm, put his thumb in his mouth and rolled over, away from the bright light in the kitchen.

When Carly flicked on a lamp in the living area and turned off the kitchen light, the tiny apartment suddenly felt too intimate.

"He's out for the night," she whispered.

"I, ah, didn't realize it was so easy to get children to sleep," he said, for something to say, anything to break the intimacy of the room. "Celeste used to scream the house down when she was little."

"So did Maddy. But my boys have always been good about bedtime." Carly smiled as she said it and he liked the effect it had on her features. She looked younger. More carefree.

"How old are you?" he asked, needing to know.

"Thirty-two," she said, and he released his breath. "How old are you?" She opened the packaging on the massage table.

"Why do you want to know?"

"Well, duh! You asked me!"

He crouched down to help her. "I had a good reason for asking you."

"Which was?"

"Never mind," he said, straightening as they withdrew the table together. "I'm turning thirty next month."

Moments later, she had the table fitted together. "I'll get some towels and prepare the oil and then you might want to undress in the bathroom," she said.

"Undress?"

"That's how people usually have massages. Oil and clothes don't mix well."

"Um, I didn't know when I agreed to this that I'd be naked."

She put her head to one side as if considering him. "Haven't you ever had a massage before?"

Now he felt plain foolish. "No," he said honestly.

"In that case, you're in for a treat."

Adam swallowed.

"You're really uncomfortable about this, aren't you?"

"Gee, how can you tell?"

She smiled again and he wondered if he should ask to see her driver's license to make sure Carly was telling the truth about her age. "Okay, I'll put you out of your misery by telling you that you can leave your boxers on."

Adam was tempted to ask if he could keep his jeans on, as well—just this first time. But she was giving him that look again.

"Not to rush you or anything," she said, and glanced at her watch. "But I'd like to get to bed before midnight."

Visions of being in bed with Carly suddenly filled Adam's head. He fled to the bathroom.

STRANGE MAN, CARLY THOUGHT as she wiped down the massage table and set some towels on it. Then she realized there wasn't another room for her to slip into while Adam got under the towel on the table. Some men didn't mind her seeing them in their boxers, but she had a feeling Adam wasn't one of them.

Tiptoeing to the door, Carly knocked gently. When she heard his gruff acknowledgment, she said, "There's an extra towel behind the door. You might want to wrap that around yourself before you come out."

Moments later, he emerged, wrapped in the suggested towel. Not that it did anything to cover his magnificent body, Carly decided. She'd never had such a reaction to seeing a nearly naked client before. Never. Ever.

Silently, she indicated he should lie on the table. "Face-down first," she managed to say, cursing her hoarse-sounding voice.

When he was settled, she draped an extra towel over his butt for modesty.

"I, ah, usually play calming music," Carly explained as she squirted oil onto her hands, warming it, then spread them over his back. "But obviously my CDs are history."

Observing his breathing, Carly breathed in sync with Adam, to create a better energy channel between therapist and client as she worked on warming Adam's skin and the muscles beneath, starting slowly, then concentrating on specific areas.

"Whoa!" she couldn't help saying at the same time as Adam jumped. "That is one tight trapezius. No wonder you winced when you picked up Celeste."

He grunted and Carly went to work on him, smoothing

the tension in his muscles with long, soothing strokes, preparing him for some deeper work on those vicious knots she could feel beneath her fingertips.

He sighed and she smiled. Clients usually sighed inadvertently with the rhythmic motion of the effleurage strokes. As she felt him begin to relax she moved back to his trapezius, kneading the knots and the tension in his muscles, feeling them gradually ease.

Every now and then, he'd react when Carly hit a particularly sore spot.

"Why does it feel like that?" he asked.

"The knots are caused by built-up lactic acid and toxins in your tissues and muscles. Massage helps disperse them," she told him.

He grunted and she went back to working on his knots. She was just getting into a rhythm when he suddenly asked, "So do guys ever come on to you when you give them a massage?"

"That was so out of left field," she said.

"Do they?"

"Some do."

"And?"

"And I tell them the session is over. Forever."

"And if I came on to you?"

"You wouldn't."

"You sound very confident of that."

"I'm good at reading people. I had you read within two minutes of meeting you."

"Should I ask what you read?"

"You could, but I don't think you'd like the answer."

He grunted again and she moved to his legs.

Carly could tell from his posture—the unguarded moments when he hunched his shoulders—that he was protecting himself from something. She soon found some knots in his calves. "You need to stretch more," she said. "This is also caused by lactic acid. You should probably do more reps and less weights when you work out."

"So you're an exercise therapist, as well?"

"No, but I get to see the results of incorrect exercise. And then I have to fix it. You need quite a lot of fixing."

"Thank you. I'll remember that the next time I'm leg-pressing several hundred pounds."

"Oh, I *know* you'll thank me for it," she said, and kneaded a little deeper to press her point home.

ADAM HAD NO IDEA WHY anyone thought being massaged was relaxing, especially when Carly got him to roll over onto his back.

He was thankful he had two towels covering him, but he was too conscious of responding to her touch. And whatever she was doing to his toes was way too erotic!

And now she'd moved to the soles of his feet.

"What are you doing?" he asked as she pressed and stroked parts of his foot.

"A little reflexology. I can tell a few things about the state of your organs from the zones on your feet."

"Sounds like voodoo to me." Adam wanted to challenge what she'd said, but in truth, it felt strangely good.

"Not at all. It's been around a long time. The ancient Egyptians are believed to have used acupressure on the feet. For instance, when I press here…"

She pressed on part of his instep. "This area is related to your stomach. Perhaps you have an ulcer? And pressing here, on the sides of your toes, relates to your brain. Maybe you overthink things and that's led to a stomach ulcer?"

"Oh, please… You're not going to claim you can tell that from my feet." Although Adam had suffered from stomach ulcers and he did tend to overthink. Except when it involved rescuing kids and dogs from burning buildings. And if he was honest with himself, he had to admit he enjoyed having his feet massaged.

"Hmm," he murmured. "I didn't realize this is what happens during a massage. I thought it was all about long, soothing strokes."

"Depends on what sort of massage you want. Or the type of massage your therapist feels you need. Since you have no experience, I'm trying a few different things."

She moved up to his shins, working in long strokes from knee to ankle and back again. That wasn't comfortable, either. He flinched and she eased off a little on the pressure, then gradually deepened it.

"It would help if you'd relax," she said. "Try taking slow, deep breaths. Like the ones you were taking when I was finishing up with your back. You were relaxed then."

Adam wasn't aware that his breathing had revealed so much. It bothered him that she'd probably noticed a whole lot of other things about him, too.

"So when did you manage to fit in studying to become a massage therapist?" he asked.

"My husband and I married young and planned on having three children. So after Maddy, our third baby, was born I learned massage to bring in a little extra income. My home-based business was building, then I got pregnant with Charlie. I kept it up for as long as I could, but I got too fat to reach across the table."

Adam couldn't help grinning at the image of Carly heavy with child, trying to bend over a client.

Then the image of Carly heavy with *his* child filled Adam's mind. *Where did that thought come from?* he asked himself, and worked to push it from his mind.

"I went back to work when Charlie was one."

"How did you end up in Spruce Lake?"

"Long story. How about if you concentrate on relaxing and enjoying this experience instead of interrogating me?"

So, she had secrets, too, Adam surmised, judging by the way she'd cut him off. And, like him, she had a right to her privacy. He dropped the subject and did as he was told.

OH, LORDY! NOW SHE WAS stroking his thighs and it was causing him to respond to her touch in a very male way. It was far too stimulating and Adam felt in danger of embarrassing himself. Maybe he needed a male masseur? He was sure he wouldn't be reacting like this if Carly were a guy.

"Breathe," she said, and deepened the pressure of the strokes.

Adam needed to say something. To apologize for his reaction. But before he'd opened his mouth, she said, "Shh, it's okay. It happens. Just *breathe.*"

Which only made him even more tense, wondering how many other men she'd massaged had gotten erections. He didn't like to think of other men responding to Carly.

He especially didn't like the thought that some of them might have tried to take advantage of her, and experienced a sudden violent need to punch out any guy who'd reacted to her like this. Bad enough that *he* was, but he knew it wouldn't go anywhere. Knew he was too much of a gentleman to take it further.

"Adam!"

Her sharp command had him opening his eyes and looking into hers.

Bad move. The room was too dimly lit. He wished the

harsh kitchen light had been left on, but then the kid—Charlie—might have woken up.

She was standing over him. So close, her hips were brushing the side of his waist. Her fair hair was backlit, making her look almost ethereal. He started to sit up but she pushed him down, the warmth of her hands going straight through his shoulders.

"I need...to get out of here," he said, finding he was too weak to fight her. Man, she was strong. Had she cast some sort of spell on him, draining him of strength?

"Adam, it's okay. Don't be embarrassed."

"But I am and I want to get out of here."

"I haven't done your chest or your arms yet."

"And you're not going to." He tried to sit up again. This time she released him.

But when he sat up, he felt light-headed. He raised his knees and rested his elbows on them, his head bowed.

She touched his back and he flinched.

"I don't bite," she murmured.

He glanced at her and forced a smile. "No, you do far worse than that."

"Oh, come on! You don't mean that."

"I'm dyin' here."

"Only of embarrassment. Nothing terminal. At least nothing that your feet want to tell me about."

He stared at her.

She said, "That was a joke."

She fetched him a glass of water. He gulped it down, wanted more, but was afraid to ask. Strange how this woman scared him, had this temporary power over him.

"Like I said, I've got to go." He swung his legs over the side of the table, preparing to get off.

"Go where?" she challenged him. "Dinner won't be ready for at least an hour. Lie down on your stomach and let me do some more work on your back and arms. You'll thank me for it later."

He had to admit he'd liked her working on his back. Those long strokes were mighty soothing. Reluctantly, he rolled over.

He could hear her squirting oil onto her hands, rubbing them together, warming it. At her first touch, he flinched, hating himself for responding to her yet again.

"Is the oil too cold?" she asked.

"It's fine," he grunted, and concentrated on his breathing.

THIRTY MINUTES LATER, Carly placed a towel she'd warmed by the fire on Adam's back and slowly rubbed him through the fabric, soaking up some of the oil and signaling the end of the massage.

Only Adam was snoring!

She smiled. When a session finished with the client sleeping like a baby, she knew she'd gotten that person to a point of deep relaxation.

Usually Carly had to gently wake him or her. But in this case, she didn't.

She went into the bathroom and washed the oil from her hands, looked at herself in the mirror and was shocked to see the bags under her eyes. She hadn't slept well the night before, constantly waking up to check on her kids. She could do with some meditation before they had to go to dinner.

Back in the living room, she lay down on the sofa bed beside Charlie, closed her eyes and placed her hands on her solar plexus shakra, breathing deeply and slowly. Within moments, she was asleep.

Chapter Four

Adam woke feeling incredibly refreshed.

He was a little sore, but it was a good kind of sore. His stomach growled and he wondered how he'd missed dinner last night.

He rolled over and nearly toppled off the bed. It took him a moment to realize he was back in his apartment, but he wasn't on his king-size bed in the bedroom; he was on Carly's narrow massage table. And it wasn't morning; it was still nighttime. He could see stars twinkling through the window over the kitchen sink.

He sat up and took a moment to get his bearings. Carly was lying on the sofa bed, Charlie curled up at her side.

The last thing he remembered was Carly working on his back in those wonderful, soothing strokes. They'd felt so good, so relaxing... He must've fallen asleep. That was nearly as embarrassing as what had happened earlier when he reacted to her physically.

Nothing came close to being as embarrassing as that. Carly had said, "It happens," and she didn't seem perturbed. Hopefully, she thought he was reacting to being relaxed, rather than the erotic effect her massage was having on him. He didn't want this woman with too many kids and the most beguiling hands he'd ever encountered thinking he was attracted to her. Because he wasn't.

So why couldn't he take his eyes off her?

She moaned and stirred in her sleep and Adam wanted to lie back down on the table and pretend he was still asleep rather than get caught staring at her.

But it was too late. She opened her eyes, blinked and then fixed him with her clear, blue gaze.

She stretched and yawned, then rolled onto her side to face him, her hand coming to rest protectively on Charlie's bottom.

"Did you just wake up?" she asked.

He eased off the bed. Big mistake, because he was reacting to her again. He drew the towel around him and headed to the bathroom, saying, "I'll get changed and out of your hair."

Once the door was safely closed, he resisted the urge to beat his head against it and mutter, "Idiot! Idiot! Idiot!"

He wanted to take a shower. A cold one. Although this was *his* apartment she was staying in, he didn't feel he had the right. Instead, he dressed quickly, threw cold water on his face, dried off and emerged, trying to look as nonchalant as possible.

Carly was in the kitchen and turned to him when she heard him enter the room. "Would you like some herbal tea? I picked it up in Denver today. It's wonderful after a massage and helps eliminate toxins."

All Adam wanted to do was go take a cold shower back at the house. But he needed to thank her for the massage before running out. "Um, okay."

She placed two steaming mugs on the kitchen table, then sat down, one leg tucked beneath her.

Adam pulled out a chair and sat, too. "Uh, I'm sorry I fell asleep. I didn't expect that to happen."

She smiled. It seemed to light up the room and warm

something in his heart, something he didn't want to examine too closely.

"I'm glad you did," she said. "For a while there, you were wound up so tight I thought I might have to hit you over the head with a blunt object to get you to calm down."

"I prefer your hands working their magic on me, rather than any blunt objects," he said, and wished he could take back the words. He swallowed. "Ah, I didn't mean it like that."

"It's okay. Next time, I'll concentrate more on your back and shoulders. Since you're uncomfortable lying on your back, we'll leave that for later sessions."

Adam had no intention of there being any "later" sessions. Especially ones that involved him lying on his back!

His stomach growled again and he apologized. He glanced at the kitchen clock—9:00 p.m.! That certainly explained why he was hungry. Dinner had ended more than an hour ago.

"I wonder where the kids are," she said. "I'm surprised they didn't come and wake me."

Adam picked up the intercom phone to the house. His sister-in-law Megan answered. "Hey, sleepyhead, so you're finally awake. Is Carly up yet?"

"How did you know we were asleep?"

"Because I sent Sash over to get you for dinner and she said you were both dead to the world. I must say, you're a fast worker."

"Very funny. We were asleep in different beds."

"So she said, so I'll let you off the hook this time. Next time you're late for dinner, I'm coming over to check myself!"

He ignored her teasing. "Anything left for us?" he asked, then noticed Carly shaking her head.

"Of course. I kept a plate aside for each of you. Would you like me to bring them over?"

"Why don't we come to the house?"

"Because Charlie is down for the night," Megan said, "and you can't leave him there alone."

She was making it sound as if *he* was somehow required to stay and take care of Charlie. He needed to get out of there. Get back to the house. Put space between him and Carly. Between him...and Carly's magic hands. Him and Carly's lips, he thought, watching her sip the tea.

"I'll figure something out," he told Megan. "Just don't let Luke eat my share." He hung up and looked at Carly. "Megan's kept dinner aside for us. I...could go over and collect yours and bring it back for you." He indicated Charlie fast asleep on the sofa bed.

"That's kind of you," she said, "but I'm not that hungry. I have some crackers, and there's cheese in the fridge. If you wouldn't mind sending my kids back here for bed, I'd appreciate it."

"Done." Adam gulped down the rest of the tea. It tasted bad enough to eliminate toxins, but he didn't tell her that. He stood and said, "Thanks for the massage. It wasn't quite what I expected."

"I hope you enjoyed it enough to want more. I owe you a lot for the table."

"We'll see," he said, eager to get away from her. She looked far too sexy standing there in the lamplight.

She followed him to the door. "Good night, Adam. And thank you."

He turned to her. "What are you thanking me for? *You* gave *me* the massage."

"Thank you for giving me the chance to start my life over again. Thank you for saving my son...Molly—for everything. Good night, Adam."

.She closed the door, leaving him standing on the stairs. Alone. The way he liked it.

Or at least that was how he used to like it. But now he wasn't so sure.

ADAM DIDN'T FEEL LIKE facing anyone back at the house. Since he'd already slept for an hour after Carly's massage, he also didn't feel like going to bed when everyone else did. It was a good time to take a long walk in the moonlight.

Memories of that mesmerizing woman's hands and what they did to him kept intruding on his thoughts. He heard a whimper and looked down to see Molly following him.

He hunkered down, holding out his hand. "Here, girl," he said, encouraging her to approach.

She came up to him and rubbed her head against him. "What's the matter?" he asked.

He felt her feet to check if they were cold, but she'd probably only come outside for a few minutes to do her business. "Go back to the house, girl," he said.

He shoved his hands deep into his pockets to keep them warm and walked toward the paddocks.

A moment later he looked back. Molly was sitting where he'd left her. If it was possible, she seemed even sadder than before. She stared at Adam and then at the house, then back at him.

"You know your way," he said. "Scratch at the door and someone will let you in."

Still she didn't move.

Adam pulled his hands from his pockets and went over to her. "You're not seriously trying to tell me you're too tired to walk back to the house, are you?"

Molly let out a mournful howl.

"Shh! You'll have every wolf within hearing distance coming to see what's up."

She howled again.

So much for a quiet, contemplative walk. On his own. Adam knelt down, gathered Molly in his arms and carried her back to the house. She licked his face with gratitude.

"You keep this up and you'll be wearing booties like Louella Farquar," he chided her gently.

Molly settled deeper in his arms, her head on his shoulder, and closed her eyes.

FROM HER KITCHEN WINDOW, Carly observed the exchange between man and dog.

She'd smiled as Adam hoisted Molly into his arms and carried her to the house.

Adam might pretend that nothing touched his heart, but Carly knew better.

Chapter Five

When Carly woke the next morning, the countryside was carpeted in a layer of fresh snow. The snow seemed somehow symbolic, as if everything in her life had been swept clean. She and her children had a future in Spruce Lake. Carly was certain of it.

Usually her children were reluctant to leave their warm beds, but this morning they all threw back their covers and leaped out, pulling on warm clothes and boots, eager to go outside and play in the snow.

Carly dressed Charlie and by the time she'd finished, her other three children were already clattering down the stairs and heading to the ranch house to find Luke's girls.

"Slow down!" she called. "They might not be up yet!"

Carly followed them downstairs and into the stables, reached for the door and pushed it open. Her children squealed.

"Snow!"

Although it had snowed on and off since they'd arrived in Spruce Lake, the snowfalls had been meager by comparison with last Thursday's—and today's. At least two feet of fresh powder covered the ground.

Carly glanced around, looking for a snow shovel, but her children couldn't wait.

They all rushed outside and grabbed at the snow,

trying to form snowballs that, due to the dryness of the air, crumbled in their hands.

She saw Adam making his way across the expanse of snow between the house and the stables, carrying a snow shovel.

"Morning," he said, and started to shovel snow away from the doorway and create a path to the house.

Carly was grateful. Although Megan had lent her a pair of riding boots to wear outside, they were no match for the depth of the snow.

"It's so beautiful," she breathed. "And quiet. So incredibly quiet," she said, referring to the complete silence of the early morning.

She looked up into the sky, which sparkled like diamonds.

"That's snow crystals," Adam explained at her smile of delight. "The air is so dry, it does that when it snows."

Shrieking, the children kicked the featherlight snow into the air. Maddy flopped on the ground and made a snow angel. So of course Alex and Jake followed suit. "Can we go sledding today, Adam?" they asked.

"Sure," he said, pulling open the back door that led into the kitchen.

Warmth gushed out, enveloping them.

"There you are!" Sarah exclaimed. "Good morning, everyone."

Molly waddled into the kitchen and greeted each of the children, sniffing their feet and wagging her tail.

Carly's kids greeted Sarah, and then the boys returned outside to play.

Molly curled up on her blanket, obviously grateful to be back on a familiar bed. Carly noticed Adam grinding his teeth as he went back out, presumably to shovel more snow.

Carly placed Charlie in the high chair. "Why does Adam pretend he doesn't care about anything?" she asked. Apart from that blanket, she almost added.

Sarah turned from the stove and leaned against the counter. "He used to be such a happy outgoing child, a lot like Will. But when he reached his teens, he changed." She turned back to the stove. "I take comfort from the knowledge that he's in a caring profession. I think the danger, the adrenaline rush, takes so much out of him that he can't allow himself to show he cares."

Carly thought it went much deeper than that, but she didn't know Sarah well enough to say anything. During Adam's massage yesterday, she'd hit an emotional trigger. She'd backed off, not wanting to cause him embarrassment. She'd hit trigger points before and ended up with grown men blubbering like babies about emotional pain they'd been carrying around for years. It was a satisfying part of her job to be able to bring forth these emotions, but she also knew that if you pressed them to bring them forward when they weren't ready, you could drive them even deeper into denial.

Carly didn't have any more time to ponder Adam and his strange behavior because the kitchen suddenly filled with the sound of Celeste and Maddy squealing their greetings to each other. Moments later, they had their heads together over the drawing pad. Daisy bounced in, greeted her grandmother and Carly, then headed out the back door, pulling on a warm jacket. "Come on, Molly!" she called. Molly lumbered to her feet and followed, her tail wagging uncertainly.

Several of the ranch dogs raced up to greet her, barking excitedly. "Shut up!" Daisy told them.

Carly grinned. The child was so no-nonsense.

Sarah had a tray of tea and crackers in her hands. "Daisy's off to see what needs to be done on the ranch today," she said. "And I'm taking this upstairs to our expectant mom. She's having a bad time with morning sickness."

"Oh, the poor thing. Please tell Megan I'd be happy to try some pressure-point massage to relieve the nausea."

"That's very kind of you, Carly. I'm sure she'd appreciate it. In the meantime, make yourself at home. The rest of my boys and their families usually come over for breakfast on Sundays, but the snow will probably prevent that. The roads in town are chaos."

Sarah left the kitchen and Carly prepared coffee for herself and hot chocolate for the children. However, Alex and Jake were having so much fun in the snow, they had no interest in coming inside for breakfast.

Minutes later, Sasha flounced into the kitchen, complaining about her "mean old grandma," and said it was way too early to be up on a weekend. Then she noticed the snow and raced outside, forgetting her jacket.

Carly was amused that even a child raised in the mountains could find so much joy in fresh snow.

"Morning."

Carly spun around to see Cody, Luke and Megan's fifteen-year-old son, wandering into the kitchen. He was rubbing his unruly mop of dark hair. "Not a morning person?" Carly said with a smile. "Would you like hot chocolate or coffee?"

"Coffee, please," he said, and sank down onto one of the chairs.

"Look, Cody! I'm drawing a picture of you being all sleepy in the morning," Celeste said, coming around the table to show him her drawing.

Cody grunted, then accepted the coffee Carly handed him. "Thanks," he said. After taking several sips, he seemed to brighten up. He glanced outside and said, "It snowed," and Carly didn't miss the note of wonder in his voice, too.

"Adam said we can go sledding today," Alex said, dashing inside. "Are we doing it here on the ranch?"

"We can," Sasha answered him as she started toasting bagels. "But there's a fantastic sledding hill in town. We'll go after breakfast and meet up with our cousin Nick. Provided the roads are cleared by then."

Daisy breezed back into the kitchen, bringing the cold with her. "Breakfast ready yet?" she asked, washing her hands. Molly rushed in behind her, glad to be out of the cold, and curled up on her bed.

Rolling her eyes at her sister's request, Sasha flipped two bagel halves onto Daisy's plate as she took a seat at the table.

Sarah came back into the kitchen, clapping her hands. "Wash up, kids, and then sit up," she said. "Carly, Megan's not well. Would you mind looking in on her?"

"Of course not," Carly said and, after getting directions to Megan's room, left the kitchen in search of her.

As she mounted the stairs and turned at the landing, she collided with Adam on his way down. She staggered backward, and lost her footing, but his strong arms caught her.

"Sorry!" they both said at once.

Carly looked up into Adam's dark eyes and repeated her apology. "I wasn't looking where I was going," she said.

"And I was coming down too fast," Adam said. He stood there, still gripping her arms.

Finally, Carly managed to say, "Your breakfast is ready and I have to go and check on Megan."

Still he held her, staring into her eyes. "You can let go of me now, Adam," she said. "I'm not going to fall."

He released her suddenly and shook his head as if he'd been in a trance, then slowly descended the rest of the steps.

ADAM CURSED HIMSELF as he turned into the kitchen. What the hell was that about? He hadn't been able to let go of Carly. Didn't *want* to let go of Carly. He tried telling himself he was only checking to see if she'd regained her footing, but she'd done that almost before he'd reached out to catch her.

He thought he'd be safe from running into her in the bedroom wing of the house, but no. There she was on the stairs, going up to check on Megan.

He needed to get out of this house. Go stay somewhere else. Except that both Lily and little Sarah were teething, and Will and Matt had warned him he wouldn't be getting much sleep at their houses. Jack was living in a tiny apartment in town that he'd taken over from Matt. The ranch hands had their own cabin out behind the stables, but there wasn't any spare room and they liked to smoke—Adam detested it.

Since it was peak ski season in Spruce Lake, he couldn't afford to rent an apartment short-term until his posting to the Spruce Lake fire department was over in a couple of weeks. Adam was stuck between the proverbial rock and a hard place.

He'd been contented in the apartment over the stables. He had his privacy when he needed it, ate a lot of his meals alone—the way he liked it. But now that he was in the house, there was no privacy. Certainly no quiet with his three nieces giggling and Cody stumbling around bumping into things because his body had grown so fast he wasn't used to it yet. He knew how Cody felt. He'd grown fast, too, when he'd hit his teens. When he'd been just a little older than Cody, he'd…

Adam felt the bile rising in his throat and rushed out the front door into the cold, needing it to clear his head, settle his stomach.

He sat on the porch steps with his head in his hands and breathed in slowly, trying to imitate the deep, slow breaths Carly had told him to take. By the third breath, he was feeling better. Surprisingly better. But he didn't want to go back inside the house. And he didn't want to head over to the stables where he might run into Luke or one of the hands.

He decided to take a long walk, try to exorcise his demons. Wearing nothing more than jeans, boots, a warm shirt and a fleecy vest, he set out across the yard toward the lake and the mountains beyond.

CARLY FROWNED AS SHE watched Adam from the bedroom window that looked out over the back of the house. He was dressed far too scantily for the weather.

"Don't worry about him," Megan said, her gaze following Carly's. "They're all used to the cold."

Carly tried to put Adam out of her mind as she went back to gently massaging Megan's shoulders, feeling the other woman relax under her touch.

They were sitting on Megan's bed. Carly had decided a shoulder rub would be the most soothing for Megan and it appeared she was right as Megan moaned softly in appreciation.

"I'm sorry you're having a hard time with morning sickness, and that it's still on so late in your pregnancy," Carly said.

"You've never had it?" Megan asked.

"Fortunately, no. Were you sick with Cody, too?"

"Yes, but it seemed much worse. I was all alone in New York. I didn't have wonderful people bringing me tea and crackers. Or giving me back rubs."

"Is Luke pleased about the baby?" Carly ventured to ask.

"He's over the moon. It was as unplanned as Cody was, so we'll have to make some decisions about *permanent* birth control when this one comes along."

Carly laughed. "Five children! That's quite a handful. You're lucky to have Sarah to help you."

"I am," Megan agreed. "But you have four children and no one to help *you*. That must be difficult."

Carly shrugged, then realized Megan couldn't see her. "To tell you the truth, I'm used to it now."

"I…I'm sorry about your husband…dying like that," Megan said, and Carly could hear the compassion in her voice.

"Me, too," Carly said a little too harshly. Lately she'd felt not only the continuing grief, which had settled into a dull ache, but anger. Anger with Michael, for dying. And for leaving her so little to fall back on financially once she'd paid the bills.

"Do they miss him?"

"Yes. I have to be careful not to show my emotions when they start talking about him. They pick up on it and then they stop. I know that's not good for them."

"The financial and emotional strain of raising four kids alone must be very stressful," Megan said. "I feel like I should be giving *you* a relaxing massage."

Carly smiled. "I actually find that massaging others, particularly when it has such good results, calms me." She finished rubbing her fingers in circles beneath Megan's ears. "How are you feeling now? Ready to face the world?"

Megan stretched and turned to face Carly. "Strangely enough, I'm starving. And I haven't felt that way in a very long time."

Carly laughed. "I'm sure Sarah's made something delicious. Shall we go?"

Carly stood, but Megan took her hand. "Thank you, Carly. Thank you for the massage and for coming to live here with your wonderful children. I hope we can become good friends."

Carly was struck by the yearning in Megan's eyes. Surely Megan had lots of friends? She seemed close to Becky and Beth, Will's and Matt's wives.

Perhaps Megan was responding to the protective shell Carly had put around herself these past two years.

She'd tended to keep to herself as an act of self-preservation. Initially, it had been because she was so busy raising her children alone. But once she sensed that Jerry Ryan wanted to be more than just her friend, she'd realized that the only way to escape him was to move out of state. After that, Carly had been so focused on getting her children settled, she hadn't had the time or inclination to make friends, to let anyone new into her life.

"Carly?"

Carly snapped out of her reverie. "I'm sorry, I was miles away." She squeezed Megan's hands. "I'd like it very much if we could be friends."

Megan's face lit up and she hugged Carly. Carly hugged her back, grateful for Megan's warmth.

By the time the two of them got downstairs, the kitchen was deserted…except for Adam. And Charlie, sitting in the high chair beside him, chewing on a piece of bagel. Molly was fast asleep, snoring way too loudly.

"Where is everyone?" Carly asked, going over to Charlie and lifting him from his chair.

"I told them if they cleaned up the kitchen, I'd take them sledding in the town park. So they cleaned it up and now they've gone to get dressed," Adam said.

"That's very kind of you." Carly was surprised by his generosity in spending a day with a bunch of rowdy children. It seemed out of character for him.

He grunted in reply and said, "Mom told me I owe my nieces some quality time."

"Then I'll keep my kids here so you can spend time alone with them."

Adam got to his feet, took his plate and coffee cup to the sink, rinsed them and set them in the dishwasher. Closing the door, he looked back at her. "It's no trouble. We're meeting up with Will and Nick."

Carly took that to mean she wasn't invited, which was fine. She was going to work through the lists of names Sarah and Megan had given her of people who wanted to book massages. The sooner she got her business up and running again, the better. "I'll go hurry my kids along, then," she said.

"No need." Adam indicated her children stomping down the path he'd shoveled earlier, occasionally kicking snow at one another.

This was accompanied by the sound of Luke's girls clattering down the stairs.

Soon the kitchen was filled with noisy children. Carly saw Molly raise her head in protest. She shushed the children, then herded them out into the living room.

Luke's girls grabbed coats, scarves and mittens, asked Alex, Jake and Maddy if they needed anything else and then they all raced out the front door, shouting their goodbyes.

"Be careful!" Carly called after them, not that anyone heard her.

"They'll be fine," Adam said, coming up behind her with several plastic sleds slung over his shoulder.

"I'm sure they will," Carly said, and shrugged. "Can't help being the anxious mom when my children try a new activity. Thank you for including them."

Adam grunted and he went out the door. Then he turned back to her, almost bumping into Carly, who'd started to follow him. "We won't be back for lunch. Will likes to take the kids to Rusty's for burgers."

"All…right," Carly said slowly. "I'll get my wallet."

Adam stopped her with a hand on her shoulder. The sensation of his touch was pleasant and unexpected. "It's our treat," he said. "Enjoy your day."

Without a further word, he strode to a big SUV, checked that all the children were belted in and drove off.

Carly hugged herself to ward off the winter chill and watched until they were out of sight. She'd been startled but deeply moved by his kind gesture. Underneath his gruff exterior, she suspected Adam had a heart of gold. But at the moment, it was a heart full of hurt.

One of these days, I'm going to find out what's really bothering you, Adam O'Malley, she vowed, and went back into the house.

Chapter Six

By the time the children returned later that afternoon, Carly had set up nearly three dozen appointments for the coming week. Several of her regulars had managed to track her down at the ranch, as well, and booked treatments.

Carly savored a warm glow of satisfaction. She was going to get back on her feet, *and* she'd be able to pay rent on the apartment above the stables until she could find somewhere else to live.

But when she mentioned paying rent to Sarah, the older woman had told her she'd do no such thing.

Carly was out in the yard, one foot resting on a corral beam as she watched Luke working with one of his horses, when Adam's vehicle pulled up. Luke was training Cody to manage the horses and his son was doing a fine job. They both looked up and waved at her; smiling, she waved back. Thinking about the past forty-eight hours, Carly was almost thankful the fire had occurred. If it hadn't, she would never have met these wonderful people.

Then guilt filled her as she thought of the Polinskis and all the other residents who'd lost everything they owned in the fire. At least the Polinskis were safe. Mr. Polinski had suffered severe smoke inhalation and would be spending some days in the hospital. Mrs. Polinski wasn't so bad, and as the hospital had residences attached to it for the use of patients' relatives, she'd be moving in there until their son came from Miami to get them. Carly had wondered why the elderly couple lived in such a run-down apartment when both had told her on several occasions how successful their son was. Why hadn't he provided for his parents?

She smiled again as she caught sight of Molly with the ranch dogs. They seemed to have accepted her in all her oddness, since the too-short legs on too-long a body meant she couldn't keep up with them when they raced around, but at least she had sense enough to keep away from the horses' hooves.

The sound of the children piling excitedly out of the SUV distracted her from her thoughts. She turned away from the corral and went to ask if they'd enjoyed themselves. Only Carly didn't need to ask because they all talked over one another. Will and Becky's son, Nick, was with them.

He greeted Carly politely, then got swept up with the other children as they raced toward the house, calling, "Grandma!" Adam and Carly were left standing alone beside the vehicle.

He reached in the back to grab the sleds and hooked their straps over his shoulder. Carly saw him wince.

"You shouldn't be lugging anything while your back is sore," she said.

"Are you going to nag me about this?" he challenged.

"Yes," she said, putting her hands on her hips. "And I'll bet you've done even more damage to your back, because you dragged the sleds up the hill with Maddy and Celeste on them—didn't you?"

"How'd you guess?" he said, unshouldering the straps and resting the sleds against the car.

"Because although I've known you for less than two days, I can tell that you go out of your way for others. Even to your detriment. *Especially* to your detriment," she said, wondering again why this very repressed man tried so hard to hide his compassion for others. "How about coming over to the apartment and letting me work on your back?"

She noticed something flaring in his eyes. Interest in her suggestion? A yearning to have the pain in his back eased? But instead he shook his head. "I'll take some painkillers. They'll fix it."

"You can't live on painkillers! Stop being so stubborn and let me massage you."

"No, thanks," he said, and strode toward the house.

"Why not?" Carly followed him, and when he didn't answer her, she reached out for his shoulder to turn him toward her. She realized her mistake immediately as he groaned with pain.

"I'm sorry!" she apologized, contrite that she'd done the one thing she shouldn't have to someone with such an injury. "But maybe now you'll agree that your problem won't be fixed by painkillers."

"I'll go see the doc in the morning, see what he has to say."

"In case you've forgotten," she retorted, "you have that disciplinary hearing in the morning. You won't perform too well if you're in pain."

He shrugged, and she wanted to slap him. "You make me so mad!" she said, losing her cool.

"Tough." He turned back toward the house. Carly fumed that he wouldn't let her help him. Was he afraid of repeating his reaction to her last night? Why was he so intent on avoiding her?

And why did she even care?

"You care because underneath his bluster, he's a good man. A man who's hurting physically *and* emotionally," she muttered under her breath, trailing him to the house. Adam might not want to admit it, but he needed her. And not just to ease the pain in his back.

ADAM WENT STRAIGHT upstairs and hunted through the bathroom cabinet, looking for painkillers. All he came up with was an out-of-date bottle of antacid.

He cursed and tossed it in the trash.

"Looking for this?" he heard Carly say from behind him, and spun around.

Was there *no place* in this house that was safe from her?

She held up a bottle of ibuprofen. He reached for it, but she whisked it away. "You can have two, on condition that you let me massage you."

"Have you always been such a nag?" he demanded.

"It's called negotiation. It's an effective parenting tool."

"Except I'm not one of your kids," he said. "Thank God."

Carly ignored the dig. "You're sure acting like one." She tipped two pills into her hand. "Now open wide," she said, unable to resist teasing him.

Adam set his mouth in a firm line. Then he pushed past her to get out of the bathroom.

"Where are you going?" she asked.

He pulled his keys from his jeans pocket. "To the supermarket. To buy a whole bottle of ibuprofen. All for me," he snapped.

"And by the time you get there, I could have eased

some of your pain with a massage. And these." She held the caplets out again, tempting him.

Adam snatched them from her and put them in his mouth, nearly choking as he tried to swallow them without water.

"My, my, you *are* in a lot of pain," she observed. "Come with me," she said, crooking her little finger.

"No." He stopped her at the door. He didn't want to go back to the apartment. He couldn't be alone with her. He needed to be where there was noise and the possibility of discovery if she got him in the same state as she had last night. With the chance that one of his nieces might burst in on him, he could keep himself in check.

He led the way to his room. "We'll do it here," he said.

She raised her eyebrows. "I hope you're referring to the massage and not something else?"

"You wish," he muttered.

Part of Carly did wish, but she clamped her mouth shut as she returned to the bathroom. After finding a bottle of baby oil, she went back to Adam's room. He was still where she'd left him, standing stiffly by the bed, glaring at her.

"What's the problem now?" she asked.

"You want me to lie on the bed?"

"That would help."

He crossed his arms. "I don't want to."

Carly almost laughed until she remembered his embarrassment when she'd first massaged him.

"Since you're probably still a bit tender from yesterday's massage, I thought you might like an Indian head massage instead."

"And how will that help my back?" he asked.

"I'm hoping it'll relax you and diminish some of that

tension you're carrying around on those broad shoulders of yours."

"Don't make fun of me."

She put the bottle of oil on the dressing table. "How am I making fun of you?"

"Talking about my broad shoulders as if there's another meaning. A sarcastic one."

Carly shook her head. "Trust me, there *is* no other meaning. You have broad shoulders." Mighty nice broad shoulders, she thought to herself. Shoulders a girl wouldn't mind leaning on. "If I'd referred to your dark eyes, would you have found something sinister in that, too?"

Adam shrugged the shoulders in question. "Guess not. So where do we do this, uh, Indian massage?"

Carly drew the tiny stool out from under the dressing table. "Right here," she said, indicating he should sit down.

He did.

"You might want to take your shirt off. There's some shoulder work involved in this and I'd hate to get oil on it," she explained.

ADAM STOOD AND STARTED to unbutton his shirt facing away from Carly. Then something perverse in him made him turn around and finish unbuttoning it right in front of her perky little nose. So she liked his broad shoulders, did she? Then she could get a good look at them—*and* his chest.

Adam saw Carly swallow as he removed his shirt. Whether she liked it or not, the woman was responding to him. It gave him a much-needed sense of power— something he felt he had very little of when he was around her. The situation between them seemed unequal, with all the control on *her* side. Carly was so self-assured, nothing seemed to phase her—except when he challenged her and then he could see the fire in her eyes. He liked seeing that fire. But right now her eyes were focused on his chest as if she couldn't drag them away.

He cleared his throat and smiled to himself when she blinked before regaining her composure.

"I believe you were going to massage my head...not my chest," he said, teasing her, loving how flustered she got.

"I was... I am!" she said, and pressed him down onto the stool.

She was close enough that if he reached out his arms, he'd be able to clasp her butt and pull her down to straddle him.

Now Adam found himself swallowing. The thought of Carly's legs wrapped around his waist, his big hands pulling her tight little butt against him, had him reacting in exactly the way he was trying to avoid.

Carly placed her hands on his forehead. He jolted at their unexpected warmth and then he was aware of her fingertips running back through his hair in strong strokes, all the way to the nape of his neck. She left them there and, using her thumbs, rotated them below each ear as her fingertips stroked his neck.

Adam closed his eyes and sighed, then instantly regretted giving Carly any hint of the pleasure her clever fingers were bringing him, of how much her touch affected him. She repeated the action and it was more than soothing, it was positively erotic.

If the door to his room had been closed, he would have drawn her onto his lap....

He wanted to open his eyes and look into hers, but was afraid of what he'd see there. Loathing—that he could react to her so easily? Fear—because she'd read his mind? Ridicule—that he was so quickly seduced by her touch?

No, never ridicule. Carly took her profession seriously. She'd never take advantage of a client. Never laugh at anyone's reaction to her.

His fingers itched to clasp her hips, pull her close. He sighed again and cursed himself for being so vocal, but he couldn't help it. What Carly was doing to him was the best thing he'd felt in a hell of a long time. Yes, the massage last night had been great, but a lot of it had been downright painful. This, on the other hand, was so incredibly soothing, so unbelievably *good,* that it was almost better than sex—

"I'll have what he's having."

Adam was torn from his erotic haze by Luke's voice. He glanced up to find his brother lounging against the doorjamb, arms crossed.

To her credit, Carly didn't miss a beat. She continued the soothing movements, shaping her hands to his head as she spoke to Luke.

"I have an appointment book downstairs on the living room table. If you'd like to fill in a time that's convenient, I'd be happy to oblige."

Adam could hear the smile in her voice. In fact, she seemed to be teasing Luke. Flirting with him. Adam didn't like it.

"And where would we do it?" Luke asked, sounding downright suggestive to Adam. He was almost tempted to get off the stool and punch his brother's lights out. Instead, he clenched his hands into fists and forced himself to keep his anger in check.

Luke started to advance into the room, but Carly held up her hand.

"For a massage to be effective, the client needs total

quiet and no distractions. Would you close the door when you leave, Luke?"

Wow. That was telling him. Luke didn't appreciate being told what to do, especially in his own house. But his brother saluted her, turned on his heel and left the room, shutting the bedroom door.

"I hope you don't mind me shooing him away like that," Carly said, her voice uncharacteristically uncertain. "But I want you to have the most beneficial treatment possible. You've got a big day ahead of you tomorrow."

Adam wanted to take her in his arms and hug her tight for caring so much. The massage was exactly what he'd needed. At least while he was thinking of seducing Carly, he wasn't worrying about the disciplinary hearing in the morning.

She stepped closer to him and increased the pressure of her fingers on the back of his head, causing his head to drop forward and rest against her midriff. She drove her fingers lower to his shoulders, kneading them, first in gentle strokes and then stronger. And just as it got almost unbearable, her hands would return to his head, soothing him, sending him into a deep sense of relaxation.

And then her hands touched his shoulders in a different movement and suddenly all the sadness and the shame he'd been holding inside over Rory began to surface. He gulped, shocked by his reaction, powerless to stop the feelings crashing in on him. Tears burned behind his eyes. Why now? Why after all these years?

And then a sob escaped his throat and, before he knew it, the tears he'd been holding back coursed down his cheeks.

With his forehead resting against Carly's chest, Adam couldn't stop the tears. Carly's touch turned soothing again, stroking through his hair. But the change in her touch only made it worse. Mortified, he raised his hands to cover his face.

"Stop. Please, stop," he begged, fighting tears, fighting the memories that kept surfacing, consuming him, threatening to drown him in all their vivid horror.

"It's okay, Adam." Carly's voice was soft.

But in his present state of mind, her words sounded patronizing to his ears. It wasn't okay. It would *never* be okay.

He sprang to his feet and caught her wrists. He read the shock in her eyes. God only knew what he must look like, a man of six-three with tears streaming down his face.

He lashed out at her verbally, trying to cover the embarrassment at his reaction to those long-ago memories. "Don't touch me. Don't *ever* touch me again!" he said, and released her so suddenly she stumbled backward.

Then he grabbed his shirt, strode to the door, tore it open and left the room.

CARLY REGAINED HER FOOTING before she landed on Adam's bed.

She hadn't expected him to react so vehemently to her finding that trigger point. Usually a patient bawled for a bit, then admitted what had set him or her off. But not Adam. Adam was too proud, too shut down, to admit his pain.

She'd guessed she was getting close shortly before Luke interrupted. Adam had been so relaxed. When he'd sighed, she'd been pleased that he was so at ease.

And then she'd hit that trigger point and felt him tense, knew he was holding back. But she'd pressed on, hoping to help him find some release from the emotional pain. But he'd fought every one of those tears until he could fight them no longer.

Carly was sorry now that she'd pushed Adam so far. She'd embarrassed him. Their session shouldn't have ended this way. She'd never had a client grip her wrists and tell her not to touch him again!

She should recommend another massage therapist, one with whom he'd feel more comfortable letting down his guard. Only problem was, she didn't want to share Adam with anyone else, didn't want someone else to help him unlock his secrets.

Carly sat on the stool, placed her elbows on the dressing table and clasped her hands beneath her chin as she gazed into the mirror. Had she inadvertently caused him to relive some emotional damage that would affect him negatively during the disciplinary hearing tomorrow? She hoped not!

Most importantly, she wondered, what could she do to make things right between them?

One thing was for sure; Adam would be steering clear of her for quite some time.

Carly opened one of the dresser drawers, found a pen and notepad and carefully composed a note to him.

She signed it *C,* folded the piece of paper and wrote his name on the outside. Then she propped it on Adam's pillow and silently left the room.

"DAMNED INTERFERING woman!" Adam muttered as he strode downstairs, pulling his shirt on and doing up the buttons with unsteady fingers. Avoiding any of the family, he grabbed his coat, wrenched open the front door and headed to his vehicle. Moments later, he peeled out of the ranch, stopping at the crossroads that led to town.

Cursing himself for what he was about to do, he turned left onto the road, headed away from town. He needed to be on his own, to think. To plan. Because he'd never know any peace until he'd confronted the biggest fear of his life.

The reason he hated himself so much.

Chapter Seven

"You and my little brother making friends?"

Carly almost jumped out of her skin. She spun around as she reached the bottom of the stairs. Luke was leaning against the wall, assessing her.

She placed her hand over her heart. "Sheesh, Luke! You scared me half to death!"

He pushed away from the wall and came to stand in front of her. "I have a feeling you don't scare too easily, but I'll make my apologies, anyway." He inclined his head toward the front door. "So what did you do to Adam to have him taking off like his butt was on fire?"

Carly had no intention of telling Luke something that was so deeply personal to Adam.

"Want to try an Indian head massage for yourself?" she said. "Then maybe you'll find out."

He cocked his head to one side. "Hmm, I don't think that was the cause. Anyway, I came looking for you to thank you for helping Megan." He thrust his hand through his short hair. "I didn't realize that pregnancy could be so hard."

"You're talking about hard for Megan, aren't you? Not yourself?" she asked with a smile.

"Yeah. Well. It's hard for me to watch her being so sick.

Apparently, she was this sick with Cody, too. I feel bad I couldn't be there for her."

Carly was touched by his concern. This morning, while Carly had given Megan her back rub, she'd told Carly how she and Luke had met, fallen in love and been separated by misunderstanding for more than fourteen years.

She put a hand on his arm and said, "You're here for her now, and that's what matters, Luke. You can't do over the past, but from what I've observed, you're a wonderful father and an attentive husband. Megan's a lucky woman."

His face brightened with a wide smile. "Thanks. You didn't have to say that, but I appreciate that you did."

"Where's Megan now?"

"Sleeping. I let her sleep as much as she needs."

"Wise man! Never get between a pregnant woman and her bed."

Luke grinned and Carly covered her mouth. "Oh, I didn't mean it to come out quite like that."

Luke grasped her shoulder and steered her toward the kitchen. "I'll tell Megan about it when she wakes up. She'll get a giggle out of it."

Carly paused before they entered the kitchen. "Luke, I wanted to let you know that my appointment book is filling up nicely. I'd like to start paying rent on the apartment, but your mom wouldn't hear of it. I called some rental agents earlier, trying to find alternative accommodation in town, but—" she shook her head "—this is high season and there's nothing available. If it's not too inconvenient, I was hoping we could stay here until something comes up."

"You're welcome to stay as long as you like, Carly. And we won't hear a word about you paying rent. It's going to be difficult enough to get back on your feet. My girls are sure enjoying having your kids around and Megan feels as if you're long-lost sisters. How could I possibly turn you out?"

Carly was so grateful, she rose up on tiptoe and placed a quick kiss on Luke's cheek. "Thank you. Megan's a *very* lucky woman to have you for a husband."

Luke scraped his boot against the floor and pretended to go all shy. "Why shucks, ma'am. You'll be givin' me a head bigger than Orion, our ol' prize-winning bull, if you keep sayin' stuff like that."

Carly dug him in the ribs. "And you can cut the country bumpkin act. I know what a good businessman and skilled rancher you are."

Luke rubbed the back of his neck. "Thank you again. But all that responsibility comes with its downside."

"Which is?"

"This crick in my neck. I didn't want to take up any of your valuable appointment times, so I thought I might prevail upon you, whenever you have a spare minute."

"Which I do now."

"You mean it?"

"Yep. Go make yourself comfortable in the kitchen. I'll run upstairs and get the baby oil." She turned to go and then looked back at Luke. "Unless, of course, you don't mind if I use olive oil?"

Luke grinned. "And walk around smelling like a salad? No, thanks!"

Two minutes later, Luke was stripping off his shirt. Carly had him straddling the chair, so she could get access to his back easily. Charlie was curled up asleep on a beanbag under Sarah's watchful eye as she started dinner preparations. Molly had her nose resting on Luke's foot.

At his first sigh of relief, Sarah smiled over at her and

said, "I have a feeling, Carly, that the O'Malley clan is going to bless the day you came into our lives."

ADAM PULLED OVER WHEN he got to the crossroads. Even now, after all these years, being here made him break out in a cold sweat. His hands shook as he let go of the wheel.

The area had changed very little, situated as it was outside the town limits. The road was still dirt beneath the snow.

He climbed out of his vehicle and froze as his gaze landed on a small memorial. The flowers were fresh. Someone had been here recently.

Adam turned and kicked the tire of his SUV. Someone a lot better than him had the guts to come here and lay flowers in memory of Rory, maybe say a prayer for him. And what had *he* done? Nothing. Nothing but stay away, far away, for the past fifteen years. Someone else hadn't forgotten who'd died here and how. But that someone didn't know the truth. Adam did. And it was eating him alive.

"I THOUGHT YOU SAID that for a massage to be effective, the client needs total quiet and no distractions," Luke griped. "So far I've had Mom nattering about what she's planning for dinner, Becky calling, Beth calling, Charlie waking up and needing his diaper changed, Daisy tearing inside to use the bathroom, Celeste wanting her hair braided and Sash and Cody fighting over what TV program they'd be watching tonight. How come Adam gets a massage in the privacy of his room and I get Grand Central Station?"

Carly slapped his shoulder playfully. She liked Luke. He had a gruff exterior, but deep down he was a big marshmallow and she liked teasing him. "Because Megan's resting and when we first came in here it *was* peaceful!"

"Someone mention me?"

Megan stood sleepily in the doorway and smiled at her husband. He reached out his hand to draw her to him. "I'd get up, honey, but Ms. Bossy Pants has me pinned to the chair. Ooh." He sighed as Carly drove her fingers back through his scalp.

"Honestly, it's been like an X-rated movie soundtrack in here," Sarah said. "That son of mine—who rarely expresses any emotion—has been moaning and groaning and sighing with pleasure for the past twenty minutes."

Megan perched awkwardly on Luke's right thigh and slipped her arms around his neck. "You must teach me some of those techniques, Carly. Seems my husband is putty in your hands."

Carly smiled. "I'd be glad to, then you can take over the orneriest client this side of the Rockies."

"Hey! That's me you're talking about," Luke protested good-naturedly.

"Sure is," Carly said, finishing off the massage on his shoulders. She placed her hands over Megan's, moving them in the same deep strokes she'd used on Luke.

Luke sighed again. "I'm glad the kids aren't here right now. This is feeling way too good."

His mother waved a wooden spoon at him. "Behave!"

"And if I don't?"

"Used to be a time I could threaten you to behave *so* easily." She shrugged her shoulders theatrically and said to Carly, "Kids, they grow up, they leave home, they lose all respect."

"Except I didn't leave home," Luke reminded her.

"More's the pity," his mother retorted with an indulgent smile.

Carly loved watching the exchange between mother and son and wondered if there'd be a time when her sons would tease her like this. She hoped so.

"You're looking wistful, Carly," Sarah said.

Carly smiled. "I was thinking how lovely it is to feel like part of your family."

"That's one of the nicest things anyone's ever said to me." Sarah wiped at her suddenly damp eyes with the back of her hand.

Carly was so touched, she went to hug Sarah, then realized she still had baby oil all over her hands.

"The next massage is for you, okay?" she said to Sarah.

Sarah nodded. "I'd like that. Thank you."

"And I thank you, too, Carly," said Luke, rising from the chair and taking Megan with him. "I'll check on the horses and round up the kids for dinner." Megan handed him a jacket; he kissed her cheek and stepped outside.

Molly lumbered slowly to her feet, following him through a doggie-door cut into the timber door that led into the backyard.

Carly stared at it. "Was that here this morning? Because I didn't notice it."

"Luke and his father made it earlier," Sarah explained.

"At Daisy's insistence," Megan said. "She blackmailed them into it by reminding them that otherwise *they'd* have to get up in the night to let Molly out."

Carly grinned. "That Daisy is one smart little girl."

"She sure is," Sarah agreed. "Daisy knows exactly which of her father's buttons to push to get what she wants."

"So does Sash," Megan said. "And Celeste is so cute, who could say *no* to her?"

"What about Cody?" Carly asked.

Megan considered for a moment. "Like his father,

Cody's a man of few words. And few demands. Their relationship was a little rocky at first, but Luke treated Cody with respect, got him involved with the ranch, taught him to ride. Now they're so much in tune with each other, it's almost scary."

Carly turned to Sarah. "All your sons are so different. Was that apparent when they were growing up?"

"You don't think each of your children is different from the others?" Sarah asked.

"To tell you the truth, I've been so focused on keeping a roof over their heads, food on the table and clothes on their backs, I've had very little time to observe them closely enough. I feel bad about that."

She thought about her children. "Alex is the responsible one, Jake is a bit of a jokester, Maddy…well, she's very much like Celeste, sweet-natured, not hard to please. And Charlie…he's my easygoing baby."

"Their personalities will become more pronounced as they grow older. Just wait until they enter their teens!"

Megan nodded. "You won't know what's hit you then."

Carly put her hands over her ears. "Please, don't remind me! Alex will be a teen in a couple of years and I'm already scared!"

"Don't be," Sarah told her. "After they got over the adolescent hormone surge, all of mine, except maybe for Adam, turned into the kind of men they were as boys."

"Why not Adam?" Carly couldn't help asking.

Sarah poured glasses of iced tea—and juice for Megan—putting them on the table, then took a seat opposite Carly. "Adam was always a bit rebellious, much worse than Will as a youngster. Then, when he was fifteen, his best friend died in a car accident. Adam was the passenger, and he survived."

"That's tragic," Carly said as a thought occurred to her.

Could memories of the accident have been what set Adam off earlier?

"I didn't know about this," Megan was saying.

"It's not something we ever talk about. Adam spiraled into a very deep depression. He flunked that year, and then when he finished high school, he couldn't wait to go to college, move away from the area."

Now Carly was starting to understand some of Adam's behavior this afternoon. Did he feel guilty that he'd survived and his friend didn't? Was he experiencing survivor guilt?

Until Adam dealt with it, he'd never be free of the demons that so obviously tormented him.

"That's why we built the apartment over the stables," Sarah told them. "We wanted Adam to return home. To give him his own space. But he wouldn't come. When they had a short-term vacancy at the local fire department, I had to practically blackmail him to take it."

And now, because he'd ignored his chief's orders and gone back into the building to rescue Molly, his job was in jeopardy. Possibly his career. Carly pondered the reality of that. Had Adam chosen a career that would require him to risk his life? To somehow make amends for his surviving while his friend hadn't? To save others, because he couldn't save his friend?

Carly put aside her thoughts as the kitchen filled with children, all rushing inside to wash up for dinner. They brought with them the crispness of the winter afternoon; it radiated from their bodies and had turned their cheeks red. Molly followed a few minutes later, her black nose pushing its way through the doggie-door. She eased her body slowly through the opening and waddled to her blanket. She looked so terribly sad that Carly sat on the floor beside her and massaged Molly's long spine. "Are you missing your mom and dad, sweetie?" she asked.

It was hard to tell, since Molly always looked melancholy, even when she was wagging her tail. She licked Carly's hand.

"Any news on the Polinskis?" Sarah asked.

"I called them earlier. Mrs. P. is doing fine, but as you know, Mr. P. suffered severe smoke inhalation. They're both concerned about Molly. I wish I could take her to visit them in the hospital. They're so worried about her future, even though I've tried to reassure them she'll always have a home with me."

"I think you've got more than enough dependents," Sarah pointed out.

Carly sighed. "I know. But what else could I say?"

CELESTE AND MADDY WERE the first ones back in the kitchen and, without being asked, started setting the table. Sasha and Cody still hadn't settled their argument over which television program they would watch after dinner. Since there was only one TV set in the house, this was apparently an ongoing debate. Carly wondered if she should offer to let one of them watch their program at the apartment, but Sarah must've guessed her intent and shook her head in warning.

"Neither of you will be watching anything tonight. Your father and Uncle Adam have reserved spaces on the sofa to watch the hockey game together," Sarah told them.

This news was greeted by pouting from Sasha and a grunt from Cody. The other children didn't seem to care. Carly soon found out why. Maddy had invited Daisy and Celeste to watch a Disney DVD in the apartment.

"But I'm the oldest!" Sasha protested. "*I* should get to choose what we watch."

"No, you're not. I am," Cody reminded her.

"And you're both acting like two-year-olds," Megan said. "If you don't stop pouting, Sash, and you don't stop stomping around, Cody, you can both go to bed without dinner *or* television!"

"That's tellin' 'em," Daisy said with a nod.

"Why can't we have another TV?" Sasha demanded of her father as he came in the door.

"Because there's enough noise in this house already," he said, and touched the end of her upturned nose.

"We'd be quieter if we each had a TV of our own."

"Don't even go there, Sash. You know how your mother and I feel about family time."

Sasha put her hands on her hips. "You mean the *family time* you'll be using to watch the game?"

"Uh-huh," Luke agreed.

Sasha stamped her foot.

"Before you say anything else, Sash, let me remind you that the penalty box applies to stomping feet as well as cussing."

"Oh, you!" Sasha said, and dashed off. They could hear her yelling from the stairs, "Just you wait! I'm gonna get a job at the burger joint and save up and buy myself the biggest TV I can afford. Then I'm gonna turn it up so loud, you won't be able to hear yourself think!"

Luke went to the fridge to get a beer. "So how was the rest of everyone's day?" he asked, completely ignoring Sasha's threat and refusing to react to it.

With Sasha's departure, the room was considerably quieter. Celeste and Maddy, having finished setting the table, went to play with their dolls. Daisy produced a deck of cards and sat with Alex and Jake. She proceeded to deal the cards for Texas Hold'em, a game she'd been teaching them. Carly washed her hands after massaging Molly, then set up Charlie's high chair and warmed his supper in the microwave.

As she fed her son, surrounded by family noises in the kitchen, Carly felt a deep contentment. Even Sasha's tantrum hadn't disrupted the family routine of preparing for a meal. Her own children rarely threw tantrums and she put Sasha's down to a combination of teenage hormones and her rather dynamic personality. She'd admired Luke's handling of it and filed it away for future use.

ADAM DIDN'T RETURN for dinner or to watch the game. Carly gathered her children together and herded them back to the apartment. Long after they'd turned in, Carly lay in bed staring at the ceiling and hoping Adam was okay, until she finally heard his SUV pull into the yard.

Relieved that he was finally home and safe and that he'd soon read her note, she slept.

Chapter Eight

The house was in darkness when Adam got home. The only sign of life was Molly struggling to her feet to join him in the kitchen. She looked at him balefully, then waddled to the back door.

She pushed her way through the doggie-door Adam was sure hadn't been there this morning.

He stepped out on the back porch to keep her company.

Minutes later she waddled back, looked at him sadly and went in through her little door. Adam stayed outside for a bit, looking at the night sky and thinking about Carly. Finally he returned inside.

He regretted missing dinner. His stomach growled as if to remind him.

He'd gone to Rusty's and downed a couple of beers before remembering he had the disciplinary hearing in the morning. So he'd sat there brooding, and nursed a beer for the rest of the night without ordering any food to go with it.

Now he was sober and hungry. He searched in the fridge, but didn't have to go far. His mom had left a dinner plate covered in cling wrap and his name printed neatly on a Post-it note.

Too hungry to bother reheating it, he wolfed it down cold. Molly watched Adam as he ate. Finally, with an enormous sigh, she rested her head on her paws and closed her eyes.

After stooping to pet her, he rinsed the empty plate and put it in the dishwasher. Adam was more than glad that he'd rescued Molly. If he had to do it over, he'd do exactly the same thing. Probably not what the disciplinary board wanted to hear, but it was the truth.

Matt had told him he'd located the Polinskis' son and daughter-in-law in Florida and the old couple would be going back there to live. As he climbed the stairs to his room, Adam was surprised by how empty he felt at the thought of Molly not being in the kitchen one morning soon.

He entered his room and, without turning on the light, stripped off, wrapped a towel around himself and headed for the shower.

Back in his room, he pulled on fresh boxers and slipped beneath the covers, looking forward to the blessed oblivion of sleep.

But something scratched the side of his face. He reached up and found a piece of paper. He was about to throw it on the floor when he suddenly needed to know what it was.

He switched on the bedside lamp and glanced at it. *Adam* was scrawled in a neat hand on the folded sheet of paper.

He had a feeling he knew exactly who it was from. Tempted again to dispose of it, he also knew he wouldn't get any sleep without reading the contents.

He opened it.

Adam, I'm sorry if I upset or offended you. Please know that wasn't my intention. If you need to talk, I'm a good listener.
C.

Adam stared at the note. Carly didn't have to apologize; she hadn't offended him. And yeah, she probably was a good listener, but there was no way he was going to talk to her about what had upset him. He wasn't going to talk to *anyone* about that. Ever.

He'd thought that by going out to the intersection today, he'd be able to lay some of his demons to rest. But it had only served to bring back all the old memories, all the good times he and Rory had shared. Closely followed by the knowledge of how badly he'd betrayed his friend.

He needed to make amends, but how? He'd believed that by devoting himself to public service, putting his life on the line for others, would make a difference. Honor Rory's memory somehow. Rory was the one who'd always wanted to be the firefighter, not Adam.

But it hadn't made any difference. He still felt hollow. Still felt the guilt right down to his bones.

He brought the note Carly had written to his nose and sniffed it, hoping it smelled of her. But all he got was a noseful of the scent of baby oil. She sure was one hell of a masseuse. Those hands of hers should be registered as dangerous weapons, considering how easily she'd got him into a state of relaxation. And then to a state of blubbering like a baby. How had she done that?

He'd been about to pull her onto his lap, explore where the chemistry between them was going, when Luke had interrupted. By the time he'd returned to the sensuous zone he'd been in before the interruption, Carly had touched something in his shoulders, and his body had given an enormous shudder. Within moments, he was reliving the night Rory had died. Reliving the terrible dreams that had plagued him too often since. And tonight would probably be no exception.

The one night he needed a good night's sleep, he'd

blown it by staying out way too late. He'd be in no condition for the hearing. Was this some self-fulfilling prophecy? Had he deliberately sabotaged himself?

He tried to push the demons aside. *Think of Carly,* his internal voice chanted. *Think only of Carly.*

He forced his breathing to slow as he lay back, hands pillowed behind his head, and pictured her. Strange how relaxed that made him feel. Then her touch... No, not good, he decided as his heart rate increased.

If he was honest with himself, Carly was his teenage fantasy come to life. Pity he hadn't met her back then.

Adam wondered what it would be like to kiss her. Make love to her. He'd had his share of lovers. Women who didn't want to probe too much, women who cared more about his body and how he could pleasure them than about Adam O'Malley, the man.

That was how Carly was different. She probed and she nagged and didn't give up until she'd made him *feel.* Until she got him so mad at her that he'd lashed out, acted as if it was all her fault that he'd lost his composure. When he knew it was quite the opposite.

He punched the pillow and tried to find a more comfortable position. He had to stop thinking about Carly or he wouldn't get any sleep. But he wanted her. More than he'd ever wanted any woman in his life.

Adam longed to throw back the covers and stride over to the stables—barefoot in the snow, if necessary—and tell her he wanted to kiss her, tell her he needed to feel her touch again.

He scraped a hand through his hair. He'd messed up so badly, in so many aspects of his life. He was damaged goods. Carly had enough to deal with; she didn't need his baggage added to her responsibilities. It would be best if she stayed a teen fantasy, rather than an adult reality.

But try as he might, he couldn't get her, or his need for her, out of his mind.

He rolled over and stared at the digital clock on the nightstand. Tomorrow already. Great. In a few hours he'd know his future. Either he still had a job or he'd lost his career altogether and would have to start over. How could he ever honor Rory's memory then? How could he ever win Carly's heart?

ON MONDAY CARLY WOKE before dawn. She hadn't slept well worrying about Adam and the outcome of today's hearing.

By the time she'd got the children dressed for breakfast—while they all chattered about what they'd be doing during their week off school—and herded them over to the ranch house, Adam was already walking out the front door to his vehicle.

She'd hoped to have a private moment to talk to him before he headed out this morning, but that wasn't going to happen now. Not with her kids hanging on every word.

Adam was wearing his dress uniform. How incredibly handsome and downright sexy he looked, Carly mused, recognizing how appropriate Adam's career was for someone of such strength and fluid grace. He was born to be a firefighter.

He got to his vehicle and pulled open the door. *Look at me,* she begged silently, and was surprised when he glanced across the yard at her.

She raised her hand to wave at him and smiled. He didn't smile back, just nodded his head as if he felt he had to acknowledge her, then climbed into his vehicle and started it.

Carly couldn't let him go like this, without saying something, offering a word of support. "Go into the house, kids," she said, handing Charlie to Alex. She cut across the snow-covered yard to Adam, praying he wouldn't drive off and leave her there.

His dark eyes held hers as she neared his vehicle. He lowered the window.

"Hi," she said, feeling suddenly awkward. Ultimately she was the cause of Adam's predicament. If she hadn't left her children with an unfamiliar babysitter, if she'd been home when the fire started, she'd have gotten all her kids out and Adam wouldn't have had to risk his life saving Charlie. He'd have had more time to rescue Molly, without having to disobey his chief's orders when the fire became too intense.

"Hi," he said back.

Carly could read the pain in his eyes. Something far worse than today's hearing was tearing at his guts. She wanted to comfort him, to impart her own strength.

She lifted her hand and touched his cheek. He closed his eyes momentarily, then opened them and gazed into hers. What agony she could see in their depths. When she stroked his cheek, Adam opened his mouth and caught the base of her thumb between his lips. Carly wanted to weep. He was reaching out to her at last.

"Whatever the outcome today, Adam," she murmured, "I want you to know you're the bravest, most selfless person I've ever met."

Close to tears, she stood on tiptoe, leaned in and kissed his lips.

"Matt, what can I do to help Adam?" Carly asked when she put a call through to him after breakfast.

"Not a lot, I'm afraid. It's up to Adam to present his case, explain what he did and why. Particularly why he ignored orders."

"It won't go well, then?"

She could hear his sigh. "I'm afraid not."

"Would…would I be permitted to attend?"

"I don't see why not. Things like this are a matter of public record."

"Then I have an idea. Would you help me please, Matt?"

ADAM HAD STRICTLY FORBIDDEN any of his family from attending the hearing. Sarah had told Carly this over breakfast. The poor woman had been in tears.

Carly figured she wasn't *family,* so Adam's edicts didn't apply to her.

After Will had collected the older children for a day out and dropped off his daughter, Lily, with his mom, Carly told Sarah what she planned and asked her to look after Charlie until she returned. Sarah was only too happy to agree.

"Good luck, Carly. And God bless you," she said as she saw her off five minutes later. Sarah and Mac were lending her one of the ranch vehicles, an almost-new minivan.

"I'll do my best," Carly assured her, wondering if she'd be thrown out of the hearing. If not by the panel, then by Adam.

Matt met her outside the town hall. They soon found the room the hearing was being held in.

Her heart in her throat, she pushed open the door and stepped inside. Matt followed her and sat beside Carly, five rows from the front. The only people present were the members of the board, numbering seven, who sat above the rest of the room's occupants. Adam was standing at a lectern facing them.

He looked so alone. Carly wished she'd notified the paper about the hearing, have some citizens who'd support Adam turn up. But he was so intensely private, Carly knew he would've hated anyone else in the town knowing about the hearing—no matter which way it went.

The disciplinary board consisted of six men and one woman. Carly didn't spend too long pondering the sexual bias of the board; she only hoped each and every one of them had a heart a tenth the size of Adam's. If they did, then she had a chance.

Correction: *Adam* had a chance.

She recognized several officials from the night of the fire. Another man, wearing a robe with an ermine-lined collar and a huge chain of office around his neck, Carly guessed to be the mayor—the owner of the pig she'd seen at the fire and who'd had her photo in the paper, kissing Adam. She smiled at the memory and hoped his pig's affection for Adam would sway the mayor in his favor. But the mayor was obviously eccentric, so who knew how he'd react?

The lone woman looked seriously scary in a dark gray suit, glasses perched on the end of her nose and lips thinned as she listened to Adam.

Then she spoke and Carly's blood froze at her words. "We keep coming back to the same point, Mr. O'Malley. You deliberately disobeyed a direct order from your commanding officer. You could have put others' lives at risk—"

"But I didn't," Adam interrupted, perhaps a little injudiciously, Carly thought.

If it was possible, the woman's lips thinned even more, but Adam continued before she could speak again. "I don't know how many times you want me to agree that yes, I did disobey an order. And I'm sorry about that. But as I keep telling you, I knew none of the other firefighters would disobey the chief by following me in."

"You sound very sure of that," she said. "Too sure and too reckless. I don't think these are the qualities we need in a firefighter in this town. Or anywhere in the state of Colorado, for that matter."

Several other heads nodded in assent.

Carly was terrified. This wasn't looking good at all. She wanted to leap to her feet and say something in Adam's defense, but was afraid she'd only make the situation worse.

Matt's hand clasped hers. Should she speak now? Carly wondered.

The mayor cleared his throat. "Are we all finished questioning Mr. O'Malley?"

All seven heads nodded.

"Then if no one else has anything further to say, I think we should vote on whether Mr. O'Malley is stripped of his temporary position with the Spruce Lake fire department."

Carly leaped to her feet before she could think better of it. "I'd like to speak, if I may?"

Adam spun around and glared at her. Then he spotted Matt and glared even more fiercely.

Undaunted, Carly stepped forward. "May I approach the bench? I don't feel comfortable yelling from back here."

The mayor inclined his head. The woman's lips seemed to disappear altogether and she pulled herself up to sit taller, as if that would intimidate Carly.

Carly stood beside Adam and said, "You probably don't know me, but my name is Carly Spencer. My four children and I lost our home in the fire last Friday.

"If not for the courage of—" she felt her voice breaking but pressed on "—Mr. O'Malley, I would now be a mother of three children. What he did that day was nothing short of heroic. I owe my youngest child's life to him."

The woman made shooing motions with her hands. "That's all very well, but Mr. O'Malley isn't being disciplined for saving any *human* lives in that fire. He disobeyed orders to save a *dog*." She said this as if it was the most distasteful word she'd ever been forced to utter.

"I'm sorry—" Carly squinted to read the woman's name "—Ms. Wilkinson, I'm aware of the purpose of this hearing, but I wanted to point out that had Mr. O'Malley not gone to rescue Molly, my oldest son, Alex, would have.

"He would've found a way to get around all the personnel there and gone into that burning building to search for her. And I'm sure you'd agree, an eleven-year-old boy would have absolutely no chance of either finding the dog—Molly is her name, by the way," Carly said, hoping that by giving the dog's name, she might appeal to their more humanitarian sides, "or surviving the fire."

Carly shivered at the memory of Alex trying to run into that building, but she also noticed that a couple of other board members nodded in agreement.

"Molly is very dear to Alex, to all my children. I don't know about you, but the thought of an innocent animal perishing in a fire tears my heart out.

"If Mr. O'Malley hadn't ignored his chief's orders and gone to find Molly, then my children would be having nightmares for many months, perhaps years, imagining Molly's final moments."

She cleared her throat and said, "Thanks to Mr. O'Malley's bravery, my children dream of a happy, healthy Molly. He saved not only the life of my youngest child that day, but also the life of my eldest son and

Molly. His selflessness, instead of being censured, should be praised—"

"This is all very emotional, Mrs. Spencer. But I'll remind you again, this is a disciplinary hearing," Ms. Wilkinson said.

"Yes, I realize it's all very emotional, but that's what life is. I won't go into the details of how difficult things have been since my husband—also a firefighter—died in a warehouse fire in San Diego. But I *will* tell you it's been incredibly traumatic for my children. By risking his life and saving a helpless animal, Mr. O'Malley has restored my children's faith in the human race and demonstrated that it's possible to salvage something precious from a fire.

"My children and I…" Again Carly had to steel herself against the tears that burned behind her eyes and bit at the back of her throat. "We lost everything we own in Spruce Lake in that fire. But what we gained in return is this. We learned that the willingness to sacrifice is part of the best of being human."

This time, everyone on the board, minus Ms. Wilkinson, nodded.

"Mr. O'Malley is a dedicated firefighter and I've since learned from his brother Matt—" she turned to smile at Matt "—that Mr. O'Malley has saved a number of lives during his career as a firefighter and been commended for it. Are you willing to risk the lives of future fire victims by not having someone of his caliber and outstanding bravery on your team?"

Carly had finished what she had to say, but she wasn't sure what to do next. Take a seat and wait for the verdict? Run from the building before she let her emotions surface and burst into tears? Grab Adam and kiss him soundly to apologize for possibly ruining his chances of keeping the job?

She was saved from making any immediate decisions by the mayor, who addressed her directly. "Thank you, Mrs. Spencer. I must say, I admire your passion and your desire to speak up for Mr. O'Malley."

He looked at her and said, "I also have to give credit to you for bringing the situation from a victim's viewpoint to our attention. I think some of us have overlooked how important that is."

Carly heard a hiss of disapproval from Ms. Wilkinson.

"If no one has anything further to add, I'd like to adjourn this hearing so the board can discuss the matter," he said, and rose from his seat, effectively ending the session.

CARLY ARRIVED BACK AT Two Elk just as her first client of the day drove up. Kandy Mason was an energetic sixty-something woman who'd been a friend of Sarah's for many years. They'd met at watercolor classes and, along with several other women in the group, met regularly for coffee and a chat. Sometimes they also hiked into the mountains during the summer to paint.

"I was so delighted when Sarah called the other day to ask if I was interested in a treatment. She knows I love to be pampered!" the other woman told her as Carly set up her table.

"Well, I'm afraid I don't do anything except massage," Carly said, worried that Kandy might think she also offered other spa treatments like facials and manicures.

"Oh, I understand, dear. I love massage. If I had the healing touch, I probably would've studied it myself."

Carly was starting to hope the other woman wouldn't

talk this much during her massage. She was feeling a little too raw after the hearing to deal with idle chitchat.

However, five minutes into the massage, Kandy was snoring softly. Carly smiled. Funny how some people were like Energizer Bunnies, talking constantly, and yet, once they were given a chance to relax, they slept like babes!

FIFTY MINUTES LATER, Carly had to gently wake Kandy. "That was the best sleep I've had in ages." She stretched her arms above her head.

"I have to apologize," Carly said. "You were sleeping so peacefully I didn't want to wake you for the other side, so I just continued on your back and legs. We could do the rest some other time if you'd like."

Carly slipped behind a screen she'd set up between the kitchenette and the living room where she did the massages, so Kandy had privacy to dress.

"That would be wonderful. Can I make another appointment for tomorrow?"

"So soon?" Carly asked as she poured her a refreshing cup of herbal tea. "Do you feel you got any benefit from the massage, since you were fast asleep?"

"I feel great!" Kandy came around the screen and joined Carly in the apartment kitchenette. "I promise to try to stay awake next time." She proffered a wad of notes and said with a smile, "Keep the change, Carly. It was *wonderful*."

"Thank you," Carly said. "I've made you some herbal tea." She indicated that Kandy should take a seat at the table and sat down with her own cup.

"Don't you have another customer waiting?" Kandy asked.

"I try to leave fifteen minutes between appointments so clients can relax and rehydrate."

"That's a nice touch," Kandy told her. "Not like the big clinics where you're lucky to get forty-five minutes of a so-so massage and then you're shoved out the door, barely dressed!"

Carly laughed and sipped her tea. She liked Kandy; the woman was forthright and it was easy to understand why she and Sarah had been friends for so long.

"Now, what time can you take me tomorrow?"

Carly flipped through her appointment book. "How about the same time? Would that work? I'm afraid it's the only slot I have left."

"Perfect!" Kandy said, standing. "I'll see you then. And I'll be sure to spread the word. Sarah mentioned you had a mobile massage business. Will you be doing that again? I'm asking because I was thinking some of the ladies at the Twilight Years would enjoy it."

"That's the retirement home?" Carly asked.

"Yes, my mom's in there. They have a hairdresser and a beauty therapist who comes once a week. She's brilliant at pedicures and the like but can't do massages."

"That's a good idea, Mrs. Mason. But I won't be starting up my mobile business again until my oldest three children are back at school next week and I've got a permanent and *reliable* sitter for Charlie. I don't want to impose on Sarah any more than I already am."

Kandy patted her hand. "I understand, Carly. Just as soon as you're ready, let me know. Meanwhile, I'd be happy to bring my mom here. She always enjoys catching up with the O'Malley clan."

THE REST OF THE DAY flew by with four more appointments. Two clients wanted all the details of the fire and Adam's rescue of Charlie and Molly. One talked nonstop about all her ailments, and the other about her grandchildren. As Carly wiped down her massage table for the last time and put it away and then washed up for dinner, she was completely drained.

At least all the ladies had promised to return. They'd also paid in cash and given her decent tips and the one with all the ailments said she was feeling much better than she had in a long while.

As she did her bookkeeping, Carly vowed to pace herself more carefully in the future. Five appointments back to back simply wasn't fair to her kids, or to Sarah, even though Sarah insisted she loved having a houseful of children.

If things continued to be this busy, Carly wouldn't need to do any sessions at the Spruce Lake spa to supplement her income. By comparison with her private clients, she was paid peanuts there.

Entering the kitchen by the back door, Carly kicked off her boots and put on a pair of snug slippers Sarah provided for everyone. It was a nice touch and made Carly feel even more as if she were part of the family.

The kitchen was empty apart from Molly, sleeping peacefully on her bed, her nose snuggled into Adam's blanket.

Carly made her way into the living room. Sarah glanced up with a weary smile that had Carly feeling instantly guilty. Although Lily was fast asleep, Charlie was sitting on Sarah's lap playing with her necklace.

Carly bent to pick him up. "I'm sorry. I won't stay away so long in future. You're absolutely exhausted."

"Nonsense, dear," the older woman said. "I've enjoyed every minute of looking after your little man. I'm worried about Adam. Still no word."

Carly's shoulders fell. She sat down next to Sarah, and Charlie immediately climbed back onto Sarah's lap and began to chew her necklace again. "Is no news bad news?" she ventured to ask.

Sarah lifted her shoulders. "I don't know. I've been calling his cell phone for ages and he's not answering, so then I called Matt and got told off for pestering Adam!"

Tears welled in her eyes and Carly moved to comfort her. "I'm so sorry, Sarah. I feel responsible. I hope I didn't complicate things for Adam by turning up and putting in my two cents' worth."

Sarah patted her hand. "Matt said you were magnificent. I'm sure what you did could only have helped."

"I hope so. But you should've seen the look of fury on Adam's face when he realized Matt and I were there."

Sarah smiled tiredly. "That boy is so determined to be independent. He never accepts help from anyone. I worry about him and the way he shuts himself off from everyone in the family."

"Do you expect him home for dinner?"

"I hope so. I've made his favorite—beef casserole— and the rest of the family is coming over to offer their support, whether he wants it or not."

Carly grinned. "I love how you never give up on anything."

"I'm just a stubborn old woman."

"Stubborn, yes. Old, never!" Carly found her fingers gently kneading Sarah's shoulders.

"That feels good," Sarah said. "Kandy called to say how much she liked you and how wonderful your massage was."

"She slept through most of it! But I thought she was lovely. She's coming back the same time tomorrow. Why don't I give you a shoulder rub now, before the stampede arrives? I think you need it."

"I'd love that."

"Then show me to your room," she said, hoisting Charlie onto her hip. Like Lily, he was probably ready for a nap.

In Sarah's room she placed Charlie on the bed and gave him his favorite soft toy to curl up with.

She turned to Sarah. "I think you'd benefit from a shoulder rub and an Indian head massage, so loosen your top garments and take a seat at your dressing table."

Sarah complied. At least, unlike her son, Adam's mom wasn't protesting all the way! "Now, do exactly what Charlie's done," she said. "Close your eyes and relax."

FIFTEEN MINUTES LATER, Carly could hear cars pulling up outside. "Looks like the stampede's here," she said, finishing Sarah's shoulders.

"I feel so refreshed. Thank you," Sarah said as Carly turned away to allow her some privacy to rearrange her clothes.

The children charged through the front door, bringing the chilled air with them. "Grandma, where are you?" Carly recognized Daisy's familiar bellow.

"You rest for a few minutes. I'll take care of them," Carly said, picking up Charlie, who'd woken from his brief nap and was playing happily on the bed.

"Any news?" she asked Will as she greeted him downstairs.

Will knew exactly what news she was referring to and shook his head. "I've been texting him for hours. Nothing!"

"He's probably feeling overwhelmed if the others have been bugging him as much as we have."

"We can't help caring. He's our brother," Will said. "Hi, Mom." He bent to kiss Sarah's cheek. "You're looking gorgeous as ever."

"Always the flatterer," she said, deflecting his compliment. "Carly's given me the most wonderful massage."

Carly smiled at Sarah. Her hair was still a bit askew, but Carly knew she wouldn't waste time away from her family to preen.

"What about me?" Will asked. "I've been herding seven overeager kids all day."

"And you've enjoyed every minute of it," his mother told him. "Where's your lovely wife?"

"Right here," Becky said, coming into the living room from the kitchen, Lily perched on her hip. "Will and the children made dessert. Better yet, I think it's edible."

"For an ex-ski bum, Will, you've certainly turned your life around," his mother remarked drily. "Of course, if your brother hadn't arrested you for vandalism and you'd never appeared before Becky in court—and had the audacity to ask her for a date—we would never have known about your latent talents. Like cooking. Have I told you lately how much I love you, my mischievous middle child?"

"Nope, don't think you have."

"Well, I do. And I'm very proud of you."

"Thanks, Ma," Will said. Red-faced, he went into the kitchen to join the children.

"Strange," Becky said. "I've never seen my husband blush before."

Sarah grinned. "That's because before you came into his life, he wasn't exactly in line for compliments on his behavior. Now I'm making up for lost time on that score."

"What score?" Matt asked, coming into the room.

"Never mind!" Sarah and Becky said at once.

"Any word?" Sarah asked.

"Nothing. And he's still not answering his cell."

Carly's heart fell. Where could Adam be? Had the outcome of the hearing been bad?

Matt tried to call him once more, but failed to make contact. When he'd disconnected, he said, "Maybe we'd better start dinner. If he comes home and finds us all sitting around staring morosely at the tablecloth, it'll make him feel worse."

Carly was all for eating. She'd been so busy, she'd missed lunch and now her blood sugar was low.

"I'll feed the kids and get them ready for bed," Sarah said. "Perhaps by then Adam will be home, or we'll have heard from him."

"Good idea," Becky agreed. "It might be best if the kids aren't around when he gets home. The last thing he'll want is a bunch of ruffians jumping all over him."

Within moments the children were taking their places at the table. They'd apparently all agreed to watch the same thing that evening, since Will had rented a recent DVD.

Carly put Charlie in his high chair and started feeding him the casserole Becky had dished up.

"Can we watch it at our place, Mom?" Alex asked. "There's a bigger TV there."

Carly had been surprised about the size of the television in the small apartment, but Sarah had explained that Adam had brought his set with him. Carly suspected he'd done that so he could hide away from his family.

Yet he'd barely had a chance to move into the apartment than Sarah had turfed him out and into Daisy's bedroom to make room for Carly and her children. Seemed like moving back home to Spruce Lake for a while wasn't working out so well for Adam....

"Sure," she said. "As long as there's no fighting."

"No way," Alex told her. "Will got us the latest *Pirates of the Caribbean* movie."

"That might be too scary for Celeste and Maddy."

"We're not watching it, Mommy. We're gonna play dolls," Maddy said.

Carly released a breath. "Then I guess that's all right. But nine o'clock is bedtime. Okay?"

"Aw, Mom!"

"Just because it's winter break, doesn't mean you get to stay up late every night," Will cut in. "Remember, I'm taking you to look at the night sky over at the observatory tomorrow evening. We won't be home till after ten."

"You're taking them stargazing?" Carly couldn't believe what a gem Will was.

"Sure. They have a big telescope over at the science school in Silver Springs. Since I wanted to be an astronomer once, I love going over there every chance I get."

"And you didn't become an astronomer because…"

"Too much math and sitting still. I wanted to ski!"

"Figures," Becky said under her breath, and grinned at Carly.

THE CHILDREN WERE FED and given the option of eating their brownies while watching the movie.

Soon the kitchen was silent as eight adults waited, ears straining for the sound of Adam's car.

No one was in the mood to eat. Even Carly, who'd been salivating as she fed Charlie, had lost her appetite.

Instead, she sat at the table and bit her nails, then berated herself. She'd always bitten her nails when something troubled her and lately she'd been biting them a lot.

"Maybe we should go home," Beth suggested. "We

might look like an execution squad if Adam walked in here and the news was bad."

"She's got a point," Jack agreed.

"Shh!" Matt got up from the table and went through to the living room.

He returned a moment later. "He's here," he whispered, although the likelihood that Adam would hear him in the yard was nonexistent. "Maybe I should go out and see him?"

"No. Sit down," his father said. "Let's serve dinner and pretend everything is normal."

"This feels almost clandestine," Beth said as she got up to help bring the mashed potatoes, peas and casserole dishes to the table.

Just as she and Sarah resumed their seats, they heard the front door open.

Chapter Nine

Adam wasn't smiling as he entered the kitchen.

Sarah opened her mouth to ask him how the hearing had gone, but Adam spoke first. "Can I see you outside?" he said to Carly, his face expressionless.

Knees shaking, Carly rose from the table. This didn't sound good.

She was about to follow Adam obediently out of the room, willing to do whatever he wanted since she'd probably helped put an end to his career.

His father stood and barred the way. "First you'll tell us how it went, son," he said.

"It's fine, Pop. I still have a job. In fact, they want me to become a permanent member of the brigade."

The collective release of pent-up breath could be heard around the table. Suddenly everyone was on their feet and rushing to shake his hand, but Adam shook his head. "Later," he said, standing back so Carly could leave the room ahead of him.

Carly put on her coat and gloves, preparing to go outside, although nothing could stop the chill. Why would Adam want to talk to her in private? Had she caused so much damage that it'd taken him this long to convince the board she was a madwoman and that they should ignore everything she'd said?

She stepped outside onto the porch and was about to descend the few steps to the snow-covered ground when she turned back to look at him. "I'm sorr—" she began, but Adam cupped her cheeks with both hands and kissed her.

His lips were warm and caressing, exactly what she needed after the stress of the day. She closed her eyes and drank in the sensation of being kissed by a man—a man she was starting to fall for.

He broke the kiss slowly, then kissed her again. Finally, he rested his forehead against hers and dropped his hands to her shoulders.

"Thank you," he murmured, his voice hoarse.

Carly was so stunned by the kiss and how it affected her that she quipped, "You thank everyone like this?"

He drew away and she could see his smile in the moonlight. "No, just pretty women."

"I'm glad, because I'd hate to think you kissed Ms. Wilkinson like that."

His smile grew wider and Carly basked in it. "No chance," he said, stroking her face with one hand. He slipped his other hand around Carly's back and pulled her closer. "She was the only holdout in the end."

Carly inclined her head toward his palm. "Not seduced by your charms?" Carly knew she was mumbling nonsense, but it felt so good to be touched, be held, by Adam.

"The only woman I want to seduce is you."

Carly swallowed. So did Adam.

"I guess you didn't mean to say it quite like that?" she said, giving him an out.

His eyes narrowed and he bent to kiss her again.

To Adam's relief, Carly wound her arms around his neck and returned his kiss. He hadn't intended to be so forthright, but he was glad he'd said it now, since Carly didn't seem put off by his longing to seduce her.

His lips parted and he deepened the kiss. After all the stress and anxiety of the past days, this was what he needed. Carly's kisses were as healing as her hands.

He drew back, rested his hands on her hips and gazed into her eyes. "You know when I said I didn't want you to touch me ever again?"

"Uh-huh."

"I was lying."

She tightened her arms around his neck, drawing his mouth to within an inch of hers. "That's good," she said, and kissed him gently. "Because if this isn't touching, I have to find a new definition for it."

Adam wrapped his arms around her, bringing her against him. His mouth covered hers but the sound of cheering had them springing apart.

He glanced toward the house. Silhouetted in the living room window was his family. They'd been watching every move he made on Carly and now they were voicing their approval.

He felt his face heating but Carly raised her hand to his cheek and her touch soothed him. "I think we have a few too many chaperones," she said with a smile.

"Me, too," he agreed. "If I wasn't starving, I'd carry you to my car and get out of here, maybe take you to Inspiration Point for some serious necking."

"I'd like that," Carly murmured, and kissed his throat, sending all sorts of erotic messages to Adam's brain—and other parts of his body.

"LATER?" HE SAID, and Carly could hear the hope in his voice.

She nodded and kissed him again. "Later," she whispered. "After dinner." Her heart lifted as Adam took her hand before leading her back to the house.

Adam stopped abruptly just before opening the door. Carly bumped into him.

"I'm not one for public displays of affection," he said, as if warning her there'd be no handholding in front of the family. No more kisses.

"That's okay," she said, wanting to stroke his face as he looked so concerned.

She was about to step over the threshold ahead of him as he held open the door when she felt a prickle up her spine. She glanced back toward the darkened yard. An eerie sense of being watched filled her with the same fear she'd experienced at the fire. But this time the threat felt closer.

"What's up?" Adam asked at her hesitation.

She shrugged. "Nothing," she said too quickly, and entered the house ahead of him. It was probably the aftermath of the fire that had her so jumpy, imagining people watching her from the shadows.

Thankfully, the living room was now deserted, giving Carly a moment to compose herself before facing everyone.

She slipped out of her coat, took a deep breath and strode back into the kitchen, acting for all the world as if nothing had happened between her and Adam on the porch. But the weird feeling of being observed from the darkened yard still haunted her.

They took their places at the table. Adam had barely taken his first mouthful when the questions started. "So what happened?" Will asked.

"Matt said Carly was magnificent and probably swung the decision in your favor, darling," Sarah said. "Did it?"

"Why'd it take them so long to decide?" Jack asked.

"When can you go back to work?" Matt added.

Adam chewed and swallowed and said, "Yes. I don't know. Tomorrow at six."

The occupants of the room took a moment to process the answers and then there was a cacophony of sound as they all spoke at once.

Eventually, Adam managed to tell them that the decision had been made several hours earlier.

"So why didn't you let us know?" Sarah demanded.

"Because I needed time to think, Mom."

Adam wasn't about to tell them that the whole experience had been so shattering that afterward he'd taken a drive back to the crossroads where Rory had died. He'd sat there for hours trying to figure out what he had to do. In the end, he knew.

"What's to think about?" Will said. "You overthink everything, Adam."

"If he overthought everything, he might not have saved Molly," Jack pointed out.

All eyes turned to the dog, and Will reached out to scratch her head with his foot. She closed her eyes in bliss.

"The Polinskis' son and daughter-in-law arrive tomorrow to take them to Miami," Sarah said. "Carly told me that Mrs. Polinski thought their daughter-in-law wouldn't want a dog living with them."

"That's strange," Matt said. "Because I got a call from Mrs. Jasmine Polinski trying to confirm if Molly was a pedigreed bassett hound. She wanted her papers. I explained there was nothing left of the Polinskis' possessions after the fire. She got downright unpleasant when I asked why it mattered. I have a sneaking suspicion that she intends to sell her to a breeder."

"What?" Becky shouted. "No way!"

Will laughed. "I think they'll find her mom mated with something else first."

"We could tell her Molly's already been spayed and she'd lose interest in her," Becky said.

"I thought you were a judge?" Jack shook his head with a grin. "Upholder of the law and all."

"Sometimes the law's an ass," she said. "And sometimes you've got to do what you can to keep a family together."

"Then it's agreed?" Jack asked. "We'll tell them Molly's been spayed."

Becky raised her eyebrows. "And to think *you* were almost a priest."

"Obviously not a very good one," Matt said, and raised his glass to his brother.

"This will only work until the Polinskis tell their daughter-in-law that Molly's still intact," Carly told them. "She had an appointment to be spayed in a couple of weeks."

"Is it too late to call the vet and arrange to have her spayed tonight?" Will suggested.

Becky swatted him. "You can't go and have someone else's dog spayed!"

"I feel sorry for the Polinskis when they discover the daughter-in-law's evil motives," Jack said.

"Which brings us back to the problem of finding a permanent home for Molly," Will murmured. "A home that will respect her whether her lady bits are intact, or not."

"I promised I'd look after her for them," Carly admitted. "But I was sort of backed into a corner, and I didn't have the heart to say no."

Sarah said, "She's welcome to stay here until we can find her a home. But she's not a ranch dog, so I worry she'll be left behind on those short little legs of hers."

Carly chewed her lip. "How can we stop the daughter-in-law from taking Molly?"

"We could offer to buy Molly," Adam suggested. "Although I'm hoping it won't come to that because she's going to expect a lot for her."

"I wonder if her husband knows what she's got planned," Jack said. "Maybe we can appeal to his humanitarian side?"

"Spoken like an eternal optimist," Luke mumbled.

"We'll put plan A into place tomorrow morning when the Polinskis' son and daughter-in-law turn up," Will said.

"What plan?" Jack asked.

"I haven't thought of one yet."

Matt held up his hands. "Much as I want to help, you'd better count both Becky and me out. In fact, this conversation never happened."

"Good point," Will said. "Mom and I will take care of the details."

THE DRIVE TO INSPIRATION Point after dinner didn't happen.

Adam was relieved when Carly said she needed to check on her kids and might make it an early night, because during dinner he'd started having serious misgiving about taking things to the next level with Carly.

What was he thinking? Getting involved with a woman with four children had never been on his agenda. Ever. He didn't want the responsibility that came with it. Didn't trust himself. And Carly sure wasn't the kind of woman to indulge in a casual affair.

He'd been thinking with another part of his anatomy when he kissed her on the porch, and it wasn't anywhere close to his brain.

The excuse that she needed an early night since she had a lot of clients to see in the morning suited him just fine.

Although he sensed that Carly was as relieved as he was when he hadn't protested.

Anything had to be better than staying at the ranch, seeing Carly every day. Wanting her... Wanting her like he'd never wanted any woman before.

CARLY HEADED TO THE apartment over the stables, thankful that she had a plausible reason for not going to Inspiration Point with Adam. Lord knew what trouble she'd end up in if she did!

She'd only been with one man in her entire life. And although Adam would probably be a wonderful lover, Carly knew they didn't have a future. She had too many responsibilities; he had too many hang-ups.

Carly didn't have room for another person in her life. Another person with even more baggage than she had.

WHY HAD HE KISSED HER on the porch like that? Adam wondered. The woman was bewitching him, getting under his skin like no other woman ever had. What *was* it about her? She was everything he didn't need—an eternal optimist, an idealist, a woman with too many kids, too many responsibilities. And yet...she was a free spirit. He almost resented the way she could pick herself up after misfortune, the way she could smile and light up a room as if she didn't have a care in the world.

At least he'd be at work for the next two days, so he wouldn't have to talk to her, look at her, let her enchant him with those blue eyes, that ready smile.

Adam used to be attracted to girls like her in high school. But after Rory died he'd shut himself off from relationships—he didn't even attend his senior prom. He dated occasionally, but as soon as anyone wanted to make the relationship exclusive, tie him down, he was outta there. He hated that fickleness of character, but it was a way of protecting himself from having to care.

But now he *was* starting to care. He cared about Carly, her kids. Molly. He cared about his family. He worried that hearing about the night Rory died would distress them, but it was something he had to confront. No more running away.

ADAM PULLED UP OUTSIDE the mountain cabin Matt shared with his wife, Beth, and daughter, Sarah. He'd purposely waited for an hour after Matt and Beth had left the ranch following dinner. He'd given them enough time to get home, get Sarah settled. With luck Beth would already be in bed. Adam didn't want any witnesses to what he had to tell Matt.

He took a few minutes to compose himself. This was going to be one of the hardest things he'd ever done in his life and he dreaded the disappointment in Matt's eyes when he confessed the truth about what had happened that night fifteen years ago.

He climbed out of the car and made his way through the freshly fallen snow to Matt's door. His hand trembled as he raised it to knock.

Matt answered a moment later. "Adam! What are you doing here? Come on in," he said, stepping back to allow Adam to enter the house.

"Can we…talk outside?" There was no way he'd have any privacy at Matt's place. In time, he'd admit the truth to Beth, but right now he didn't want her burdened with his shame. Not until there was some resolution. The O'Malleys would have enough to endure over the coming weeks, when the circumstances surrounding Rory's death were revealed to the community of Spruce Lake.

Matt frowned, but didn't query him further. "Sure, I'll get my jacket."

Moments later, Matt joined him on the stoop and shrugged into his warm jacket. "It must be twenty below out here," he said. "What's up that you didn't want to come inside and have some tea or hot chocolate with Beth and me? Or talk about it at the ranch, for that matter?"

Adam turned away and started toward the gate leading into the property, giving Matt no alternative but to follow.

"If it's relationship advice you want, little brother, then you should be talking to Beth."

Adam spun around and said, "I killed someone and I want to make it right."

Matt stopped in his tracks and peered into his face. "Run that by me again?"

"I was the one driving the night Rory was killed."

Matt let out a long breath. "Damn," he muttered.

"I can't live with the guilt anymore, Matt. I hate being hailed as a hero, when the truth is, I'm a complete lowlife who killed his best friend and was too much of a coward to admit it."

Matt placed a comforting hand on Adam's shoulder and said, "I think we need to talk inside."

Adam shrugged him off. "I can't. I don't want Beth knowing about this yet. I can't tolerate the embarrassment. I wanted to talk to you first and find out what I have to do about turning myself in. And then…I need to talk to Rory's mom."

"Why didn't you tell someone about this when it happened?"

"You're kidding, right? I was fifteen. I was knocked out for a couple of days, and by the time I came to, the funeral was over and the accident investigators had concluded that Rory was driving. Case closed. I was scared and I didn't see any point in telling the truth—that I was in the driver's seat and thrown clear when the truck rolled. Yeah, I know it was lousy of me. Cowardly. But like I said, I was fifteen. Selfish and scared. Who do I turn myself in to?"

"Since it happened outside the town limits, me, I guess."

"How long do you get for murder?"

"For a start, it would be classified as vehicular homicide. That's a class-four felony and the usual term is from two to six years if memory serves me—"

"*Six* years?"

"You asked."

"I know. I know. On the one hand it's a shock, but on the other it seems too short a sentence for such a serious crime. So do you arrest me here or take me down to the sheriff's department or what?"

"If you'd let me finish what I was saying earlier, I would've told you that the statute of limitations on vehicular homicide in the state of Colorado is five years."

"Which means?"

"You won't be facing a jail term."

Adam let out his breath in a whoosh. "But?"

"There is no *but*. Because you didn't come forward within five years of the accident, no charges will be laid and you won't have a record."

Adam shook his head, disbelieving. "It doesn't seem right. I killed someone and I walk free?"

"You've lived with this for a lot of years.… It's torn your guts out, and I don't see that as walking free, Adam. You've led an exemplary life, saved lives in the line of duty. You've repaid your debt to society."

"Then why do I feel like crap?"

"Guilt? The knowledge that it's too late to make amends?"

"I need to talk to Rory's mom."

"And what do you think that will achieve? You'll be bringing up old memories. Maybe she'd prefer them to stay in the past."

"I need her to know that Rory wasn't responsible for his death."

When Matt was about to object, he held up his hand and said, "Yeah, yeah, everyone knows Rory was always doing daring things and everyone believed he was going to mess up his life, but Mrs. Bennett deserves the truth."

"You could be opening a whole can of worms—not the least of which is that she could sue you."

"Which would be her right."

"It could ruin your life."

"So? I've ruined hers. Mr. Bennett drank himself to death after the accident and she's been alone all these years."

"Grant Bennett was a drinker long before you were born, Adam. You can't blame yourself for his death, too."

"I can't help feeling that I contributed to it."

"For all you know, Rory could've gone down the same path as his old man. He had a blood alcohol level more than twice the legal limit, if I remember. And there's evidence that alcoholism runs in families."

"It still doesn't account for the lousy life Mrs. Bennett's led. As a result of my actions, her only son is dead."

Matt sighed. "Do you want me to come with you when you talk to her?"

Adam shook his head emphatically. "I have to do this on my own."

Matt clapped him on the back. "I admire you for coming forward, even if it is fifteen years later. It takes guts to own up to something like that."

Adam wasn't listening. "And then I need to talk to Mom and Pop."

"Oh, no! I don't think that's a good idea."

"Matt, this is going to get around town. Even if Mrs. Bennett doesn't go ballistic and sic the lawyers on me, the truth will get out. I don't want Mom and Pop hearing it from some third party."

Matt nodded. "I can see you've thought this through. I'll come with you to see our folks, then. Mom might react badly."

"I can't talk to them tonight. It'll have to wait until after my next shift at the fire station. In the meantime, can you keep this to yourself?"

Matt clasped his shoulder and turned him back toward his vehicle. "You have my word, buddy."

A HALF HOUR LATER, ADAM parked outside the Bennett residence. It was a tiny weatherboard house that could do with a coat of paint and some repairs to the gutter and roof, he noticed.

Taking a deep breath, he stepped out of his car onto Gray Street and crossed the road to Mrs. Bennett's front walk.

He paused at the rusted gate. What was he doing? It was way too late to be visiting someone. Especially when you were bringing bad news. Reviving bad memories.

He was about to turn back to his vehicle when the front door opened and Mrs. Bennett came onto the porch.

Adam wanted to shrink into the shadows. It had been many years since he'd seen Rory's mom. She'd always been slender, but now she was painfully thin. She wrapped her arms around her against the chill of the night and called out, "Who's there?"

Now she probably thought she had a prowler. Adam

didn't want to cause her any worry, so he walked through the gate and said, "It's me, Mrs. Bennett. Adam O'Malley."

"Adam! How lovely to hear your voice after all these years. Come into the light where I can see you," she said, gesturing with her hand.

On shaking legs, Adam strode up her shoveled path and onto her porch. The harsh light showed the lines on her face, but she had that smile he still remembered. Rory's smile.

"Hello, Mrs. Bennett," he said, his voice hoarse with emotion. He shouldn't have come here. He shouldn't have come to ruin this good woman's night by bringing back all the memories of the night her only son died.

"It's Jennifer, please!" she said, and hugged him. "You're much too old to be calling me Mrs. Bennett these days."

Adam hugged her back, but carefully. She felt so frail beneath his hands.

"Have you got time to come inside?" she asked, and Adam could hear the yearning in her voice, the desperation for someone to keep her company.

"Sure," he said. "I was coming to see you, anyway, but then I thought it might be too late."

She opened her door and ushered him inside. A small fire burned in the grate, barely warming the living room. "I'm sorry I don't have much of a fire. I've hurt my back and can't split enough wood to get a good fire going."

"I can do that for you," Adam offered.

"Thank you. You were always such a kind boy."

Adam swallowed down the guilt that was choking him. He wondered if he should split her wood now, before his big admission, or later.

"Would you like some hot chocolate?" she asked. "I just boiled the water."

"That would be great. Thanks." Adam knew he was being formal with her, but this was the most awkward situation he'd ever been in.

Jennifer Bennett tipped hot chocolate mix into two mugs, then filled them with hot water. She stirred them, then handed one to Adam and indicated they should return to the living room. She hastily brushed aside some newspapers opened to the crossword section so Adam could take a seat on her worn sofa.

Adam placed his mug on the coffee table. There was no way he could drink anything right now. He needed to get the words out before his courage failed him.

Courage. What a joke.

"Mrs. Benn—Jennifer, I have something I need to tell you and you're not going to like it."

ADAM LEFT JENNIFER BENNETT'S house two hours later. A lot of emotions had been spent in those hours. And a friendship forged.

It astonished him how happy Rory's mom had been to see him, how she'd welcomed him like a long-lost son. And then he'd told her what had happened the night Rory died.

She'd thanked Adam for admitting the truth, praised his courage in coming to her. And then, most astonishing of all, she'd forgiven him.

They'd talked for a long time. Jennifer had gotten out photographs of Adam and Rory together and they'd remembered the good times. Then he'd split what remained of her meager wood pile.

Guessing she probably didn't have the money to get in more firewood, he told her he'd bring a truckload around when he finished his forty-eight-hour rotation and split it for her. She'd have more than enough to keep her house warm through the winter.

In the morning, he'd order a box of groceries delivered to her from the supermarket and some flowers from Mrs. Farquar, the mayor's wife. It was the least he could do to make up for all the years he'd stayed away.

As he lay in bed that night, for the first time in too many years Adam felt the weight of his guilt pressing less heavily on his chest. But he knew that in a small house on the outskirts of town, Jennifer Bennett was mourning the loss of her son all over again.

Chapter Ten

The next morning the Polinskis' son and daughter-in-law arrived in town.

Matt had asked them to come by his office first, before they picked up the old couple from the hospital.

And while the Polinskis' son, George, was pleasant enough and grateful for everything the fire department and rescue personnel had done for his parents, the daughter-in-law was another matter.

Jasmine Polinski's designer clothes would be the envy of many a woman in Spruce Lake, Matt surmised. But the fur coat she wore would've guaranteed her being scorned by nearly everyone.

Once settled in Matt's office, she demanded to know where Molly was.

Matt had patiently tried to explain to her—since her husband had stepped out of the office to take a call—that Molly was still suffering from smoke inhalation and probably shouldn't be moved anytime soon. He then bit his lip and hinted that Molly might not be a pedigreed basset, after all.

"They told me she was a pedigreed bassett hound!" she screeched. "Her puppies are supposed to sell for over a thousand dollars each!"

Matt did his best to hold his tongue. "If she isn't pedigreed, then any puppies she might have could be very difficult to place. In fact, my brother Will, who's an expert on dogs…" This wasn't entirely true, but Will liked dogs and they liked him, so Matt didn't mind bending the truth about Will's expertise. "Anyway, he thinks Molly's mom might have mated with another dog first. I'm afraid that, in spite of your in-laws' beliefs, Will thinks she's a mixed breed." So much for his suggestion that he and Becky stay out of the whole Molly issue. But something about this woman brought out the devil in Matt and he couldn't resist baiting her.

"You mean…she's a *mongrel?*"

The word dripped with contempt and Matt hated her for it.

"I don't believe you. I want to see her. Where *is* she?"

"At my family's ranch," Matt told her. "I can take you over there later—"

"I want to see her *now.*"

Matt had no desire to let this poisonous woman anywhere near the ranch, so he opened his cell and called his mother. "I'll have my mom bring her into town. I'm sure Carly Spencer, who was a neighbor of your in-laws' and who's now staying at our family's ranch, would love to see them before they go to Miami with you."

When his mother answered, Matt said, "Hi, Mom. Would you mind bringing Molly to my office? The Polinskis want to collect her here. Bring Carly, too, because Mr. and Mrs. Polinski will be taking his parents back to Miami on this afternoon's flight."

"What's she like?" Sarah asked. Matt stayed silent. "I see. Carly and I will be there in twenty minutes. Bye."

As it turned out, they were a good thirty minutes. Matt tried to engage Mr. Polinski's son in conversation, but he spent more time taking calls on his cell phone in the corridor than talking to Matt.

Desperate to convince them to leave Molly in Colorado, Matt searched his desk drawers for a brochure he'd received from the Twilight Years last week.

He gave it to Jasmine Polinski. "If you'd prefer, your parents-in-law could stay in Colorado," he said. "We have an excellent retirement home right here in Spruce Lake. I know they allow residents to keep their dogs there. They've just completed some excellent independent living units that would be perfect for your parents-in-law."

Jasmine Polinski sniffed with distaste. "And who do you think is going to pay for this?"

"Your mother-in-law told me they own several investment properties," Matt said. Although why they'd spend their retirement years renting an apartment in a run-down old building, he was at a loss to understand.

"They can't be sold!" she snapped.

"Why not?" Matt asked reasonably, knowing the answer. The older Polinskis had said something about the properties being tied up in a family trust. Matt had the uneasy feeling they were being used as collateral for the younger Polinskis' investments—and lifestyle.

"If your parents-in-law could liquidate some assets to help make their retirement more comfortable *and* keep Molly with them, surely that would be a solution agreeable to all of you?"

"I told you the other day. They're coming to live in Miami, and the dog is going to be sold."

She was nothing if not forthright about her plans for Molly. Matt had gotten to the point where he'd decided strangulation would be too good for the woman.

"And do Mr. and Mrs. Polinski know that?"

"Not yet, but since they don't have anywhere else to go, they'll just have to suck it up."

"Excuse me?"

The woman leaned over Matt's desk and spoke in a low, threatening tone as she tapped a long fingernail on his blotter pad. "Listen, *Sheriff,* we're taking my husband's parents back to Miami with us. What happens to them, or their dog, when they leave this Podunk town is none of your business."

"Is it your husband's business?"

"He does as he's told!"

Matt sat back in his chair to put as much physical space between Jasmine Polinski and himself as possible. "Mrs. Polinski, I'm surprised you don't want Molly staying with them at your house. She's a lovely dog and wouldn't be any trouble."

"Because, *Sheriff,* they won't be staying in our house. They're going to the retirement trailer park!"

Bingo! "And they don't allow dogs?" Matt didn't believe that for a moment. "Then wouldn't it be preferable to have your parents-in-law move into a perfectly nice retirement home here, in a community they love?"

"Like I said, who's going to pay for it?"

"You'd rather drag them across the country and set them up in a trailer in Miami? Because it's *cheap?*"

"We all need to economize in these difficult times."

"Y…es," Matt said slowly, taking in her designer outfit and then gazing pointedly at her fur coat. "We certainly do."

WHEN SARAH ARRIVED WITH Carly and Molly, things went from bad to worse. Molly looked, and smelled, as if she'd been rolling in something unmentionable. Jasmine Polinski screeched with horror when Molly waddled in wagging her tail and rubbed her fat little body against her leg.

"Get that mongrel away from me!" she cried.

Molly growled at the insult and bared her teeth. Then she latched onto Mrs. Polinski's fur coat and, with a fierce shake of her head, wrestled it off her shoulders and onto the floor.

The behavior was so uncharacteristic of Molly that Sarah, Matt and Carly were too shocked to react quickly enough.

Jasmine Polinski lashed out, kicking Molly viciously in the ribs with the pointed toe of her expensive boots.

Molly howled in pain. Sarah kicked Mrs. Polinski in the shin and Carly dropped to the floor to comfort Molly.

"I want that dog put down!" Jasmine Polinski screamed. "And I want this woman charged with assault!"

Although Matt had been appalled at his mother's reaction, he wasn't sure he wouldn't have done the same thing.

"First, we don't euthanize dogs who bite fur coats. Second, I *could* charge this woman with assault," Matt said, mirroring the woman's tone of voice and earning a glare from his mother.

"But before I do that, I'm going to charge *you* with animal cruelty, which in this county is a far greater crime."

He picked up his phone and said, "I'm calling our animal cruelty officer to come down here and take witness statements. Then I'm arresting you."

"You can't arrest me!"

"I can, and I will," he said to her, and then into the phone, "Can you come to my office for a moment? I have an animal cruelty case for you."

"What's going on?" George Polinski asked from the

doorway. Apparently, he'd finally found time to attend to his parents.

Jasmine dragged her husband into the room and slammed the door shut. "He wants to arrest me!"

"Your wife assaulted an innocent animal," Matt explained. "That carries a heavy penalty. I'm presently waiting for an officer from animal cruelty to come and take statements from the witnesses."

Jasmine Polinski pointed her bloodred, perfectly manicured index finger at Sarah. "That woman *kicked* me!"

"Only because you kicked Molly first," Sarah retorted. "What sort of person are you to abuse a harmless animal?"

"She's ruined my fur coat!"

"You have no business wearing the fur of a wild animal on your back!" Sarah yelled.

His office was starting to sound like a playground, but Matt was loath to stop his mother from venting her spleen. Animal cruelty was unforgivable, and his mom was more than a match for any designer-clad harpy from the East Coast.

"I'm going to make sure the animal cruelty officer knows *exactly* what you did to Molly. There's no way he'll let her leave this town with you, you lous—"

"Thank you, ladies, that'll be enough yelling for now. If you keep it up, you'll have the prisoners over in the county jail wanting to join the fray."

"Yeah!" Sarah said. "But since she'll be there with them in a couple of minutes, they won't need to come over here."

Jasmine Polinski paled beneath her makeup. Carly concluded she must have watched some of those prison-reality programs on TV.

"Do you strip-search prisoners?" Carly asked Matt.

Obviously guessing where she was going, he nodded. "Oh, yeah."

"That's barbaric." Carly covered her mouth to hide her grin of delight.

Matt shrugged. "Gotta be done, I'm afraid. Can't tell what people have hiding on, or *inside,* them."

"But…but I haven't got anything hidden on *me!*" Jasmine insisted.

Matt grinned wolfishly, his lips pulling back over his teeth. "That's what they all say. In fact, the prisoners who protest the most are generally the ones who're hiding something. They get searched, from top to bottom.…" He let the last word hang in the air. "Sometimes two, even three times."

Carly enjoyed watching the emotions on the woman's face. She'd gone from arrogant to incensed to horrified in a matter of minutes.

There was a knock at the door.

"That will be the animal cruelty officer," Matt said.

"Wait! Don't let him in yet," Jasmine Polinski demanded.

"If you want to make a full confession, that's fine, but you'll still be charged and incarcerated," Matt warned. "Might take a while to get you bailed. Could be the judge won't give you bail. I did tell you this county looks very unfavorably on animal cruelty, didn't I?"

"*Do* something!" she implored her husband.

"Like what? Seems you're going to be locked up for the night, my dear."

Carly wanted to cheer George Polinski. Maybe he had a backbone, after all.

Jasmine bent and fished around in Matt's wastebasket

and came up with a crumpled brochure for the Twilight Years. She thrust it at her husband.

He glanced at it and said, "You have to be over fifty-five to live here. I don't think it's an alternative to jail."

"For your parents, you idiot!" she snapped, then looked at Matt. "If I...*we* agree to place his parents in this place, will you drop the charges?'

"It's not my call. Animal *cruelty*..."

"Please?" she begged.

"It's up to your husband. Would he prefer to see you behind bars? Or his parents living out the rest of their lives—with Molly—in the Twilight Years?"

All eyes in the room swung to George Polinski.

He took a good long time making up his mind.

"George! So help me, I'll..."

"You'll what?" George asked. He clearly liked having the upper hand for once.

She stomped her expensively booted foot.

"Considering the circumstances, Sheriff," George said, returning his attention to Matt, "and the fact that our lawyer charges like a wounded bull, it would probably be cheaper to place my parents in the Twilight Years—should that be their wish—than pay to defend my wife's actions with regard to Molly." At this point he looked down at the dog for the first time and frowned. "What's that muck all over her?" he asked.

Carly scrambled to her feet and rubbed her hands on the seat of her jeans. "It's engine grease. Molly's taken to running around with the ranch dogs, but she went under a tractor—a parked one," she hastened to point out, "and got covered in engine grease. I've been trying to wash it off all morning."

"I see," he said, then looked back at Matt. "I'll call the Twilight Years, and provided they have a vacancy for my parents, I'd be very grateful if you'd drop the charge pending against my wife."

"And if they don't have space for them?" his wife demanded, and then seemed to realize that was a very stupid question, given her tenuous situation. "I mean, of course they'll have room for them. In fact, I'm sure they'd look very favorably on a generous donation to take them off our hands."

TEARS OF LAUGHTER HAD flowed down Sarah's and Carly's cheeks after they'd returned to the ranch and told everyone present what had happened in Matt's office. Will had whooped with joy as he imagined Matt lying with a completely straight face. Even Luke had cracked a smile.

"So the Polinskis are moving into their new home at the Twilight Years as we speak," Sarah said.

"And Molly's staying here for a few days while they get settled," Carly finished.

"And you're going to wash off that disgusting mix of engine grease and cow manure you rubbed all over her, Will," his mother said sternly, then smiled and patted his cheek. "Actually, that was such a stroke of brilliance, I think I'll wash her for you."

"I'll help!" said Alex.

Carly had loved watching all the children's faces as she and Sarah had related the story of pretentious Jasmine Polinski and her brush with the law—and a very dirty dog. She was only sorry Adam wasn't there to share in the fun.

LATER THAT AFTERNOON, Carly took a trip to the supermarket to do some shopping for Sarah. While waiting to be served in the deli section, she experienced the same weird prickle up her spine that she'd felt the day of the fire and the other night at the ranch.

She spun around and came face-to-face with Jerry Ryan.

"Carly! I wondered if that was you."

Carly was so flabbergasted, it took her a moment to regain her senses.

"What are you doing here, Jerry?" she demanded, unable to hide her shock—or her dismay.

"Is that any way to greet an old friend? Come on, give me a kiss, it's been ages!"

Without waiting for Carly to kiss him—not that she'd intended to—he took hold of her shoulders, kissed her cheek and pulled her into a hug.

Startled, Carly had remained frozen in his embrace. She needed to get out of this without spending too much time with Jerry. Certainly not enough time for him to question her about what she'd been up to and where she was living now.

She plastered a smile on her face and drew back. "It's such a surprise to see you here, Jerry. I didn't know you skied."

"Decided it was time to learn, so…I ended up here."

In exactly the same town she was living in? Carly fought to control her racing pulse. There was no way he'd *accidentally* found her here. Carly was sure of it. She'd deliberately avoided telling him about the job in Denver. After the hotel was firebombed, she hadn't even told her parents where she'd relocated. Until last week….

"So how've you been? How are the kids?"

Carly had no intention of saying anything about the fire; he'd go all protective on her. Probably insist on taking her and the kids back to San Diego to live with him. *Not* what she wanted!

"Great! We love living in the mountains."

"You were going to email and tell me where you'd moved in Denver so I could come and visit."

She had *not* mentioned him visiting! "I'm sorry, I've been so busy with work, getting the kids settled in school…" She shrugged. "Stuff like that."

"I thought your new job was in Denver. What are you doing here?"

This was starting to feel like an interrogation. And Jerry was standing way too close. She took a step back, bringing the shopping basket up to rest in front of her, and said, "It didn't work out."

Just as she was wondering how she could get away from him before he asked where she was living now, Jerry threw her an unexpected lifeline.

"If you're not busy, we could go and have a coffee."

"Actually, I *am* busy." Carly waved Sarah's shopping list beneath his nose. "I'll have to take a rain check."

"When? Dinner tonight?"

Hell, no! Carly shook her head. "I'm sorry, I can't get a sitter on such short notice."

"I could bring takeout to your place."

Did this guy never give up? Carly could feel the walls of the supermarket closing in on her. She had to get out of there, had to get away from Jerry.

"I don't think that's a good idea. I'm…I'm seeing someone."

She saw the glint of jealousy in Jerry's eyes before he managed to get his emotions under control. "That's great! Who is he? Maybe I should check him out for you. Don't want my best bud's widow being duped by some shyster."

"I'm old enough to take care of myself, Jerry. But thanks for the offer…."

ADAM WATCHED FROM A distance as Carly spoke to the other man. When she'd kissed him, he'd experienced a jealousy that went bone-deep and left his guts burning.

He'd come to the supermarket with a couple of the other guys on duty to shop for tonight's dinner. Rounding the end of the deli aisle, he'd spotted Carly and had been about to approach her when the other guy had walked up.

Curious, he'd tried to gauge the relationship between them, but finally curiosity got the better of him.

"CARLY!"

Carly turned toward the voice calling her name. Adam! Thank goodness. She'd never been so relieved to see anyone in her life.

"Hi," he said, coming up to her. He looked gorgeous in his uniform, Carly thought. Real hero material. Funny how Jerry's uniform and even Michael's had never affected her that way.

"Hello, Adam," she said a little coolly, not wanting to alert Jerry to the fact that Adam was the man she was "seeing."

No one else needed to be dragged into her private affairs. She'd left San Diego behind two months ago, and as soon as she got out of this store, Jerry would be history. She refused to *ever* let him surprise her again.

"Who are you?" Jerry demanded rudely. Carly could practically see the hackles rising on the back of his neck.

Adam crossed his arms. "I'm—"

"He's the son of a good friend of mine," Carly cut in. Jerry's obsession with her gave Carly the uneasy feeling that if he knew Adam was more to her than just the son of a friend, it wouldn't end well for Adam.

Her eyes begged his forgiveness. He resisted for a moment and then backed down, offering his hand to Jerry. "Adam O'Malley. And you are?"

Jerry stared at his hand as if debating whether to shake it or put Adam in a headlock.

"Jerry Ryan. I'm a *very* close friend of Carly's from San Diego," Jerry said. "Now if you'll excuse us, we have some catching up to do," he said dismissively.

"Funny, she never mentioned you," Adam said, and Carly nearly groaned.

"Adam, you and I hardly know each other. Why would I discuss my private affairs with you?" She regretted the word *affairs* as soon as she'd uttered it.

Adam seemed about to argue.

Carly needed to get out of there and fast. The sliced roast beef she was supposed to get from the deli could wait for another day.

"It was nice seeing you both," she said. "But I have things to do." She turned to Jerry. "Have a wonderful holiday, Jerry. Bye."

Without giving him the chance to respond or swoop in for a goodbye kiss, Carly strode through the deli department, her head bent as she pretended to examine Sarah's shopping list. She didn't take a breath until she'd gone through the checkout and was seated in Sarah's car.

ADAM RETURNED TO THE ranch after his forty-eight-hour shift at the firehouse, but he was acting strangely. He was avoiding her, Carly decided. Probably upset about the confrontation in the supermarket.

Seeing Jerry had unnerved her. So much so that she'd decided it would be better to keep her distance from Adam—at least until Jerry had left town. Although how long that might be, she had no idea. Like Adam, he worked a two-day-on, four-day-off cycle. He could be here another three days, or even longer, if he really *was* on vacation.

CARLY'S APPOINTMENT BOOK was full. One of her clients was the mayor's wife, Edna Farquar, a friend of Sarah's. She had a massage booked twice a week, mostly to work on her neck and shoulders. From what Carly could tell, much of her tension was caused by the mayor's pet pig, Louella.

Carly remembered the sight of the pig at the fire, trotting around in red rubber booties as if she owned the place. She seemed very attached to Will, but when Carly had questioned Becky about it, she'd shuddered and suggested they change the subject.

She smiled at the memory of Louella planting a wet kiss on Adam as he lay on the stretcher. Adam didn't seem too fond of Louella, either. However, Carly would be meeting her in person—so to speak—tomorrow as Will was entertaining Louella and all the children at the ranch.

Will and Becky had an interesting marriage; Will was a stay-at-home dad, while Becky worked as a county judge. Will seemed happy to take on the responsibility of caring for Carly's children as well as his own and Luke's three daughters. He was a born nurturer and, according to Alex, had a lot of activities planned for them the following day. He was also helping the children make and wrap a special gift for their grandfather Mac's birthday. The following day, with Adam's assistance, he was taking everyone skiing.

"Can I talk to you for a minute?"

Carly jumped at the sound of Adam's voice. She'd been so absorbed in thinking about Will, she hadn't noticed Adam's approach.

"Sure," she said with a smile, trying to keep it light.

Adam, having made the request, now seemed stuck for words. He cleared his throat, then ran his hand through his hair.

"How was work?" she asked, mostly to fill the conversation gap.

"Ah, fine. No serious fires."

"Good." Carly waited.

"Um…"

"Look, if you're going to say the other night on the porch was a huge mistake, Adam, that's okay with me. I feel the same way. So let's not draw it out. You're a great kisser, but I don't want to get involved with you."

Adam looked so completely poleaxed, Carly regretted her words almost as soon as they left her mouth.

"Ah…" He shook his head. "That wasn't what I wanted to talk to you about. I was going to say I need to speak to my family in private tonight, so if you don't mind, could you make yourself and your kids scarce?"

Now it was Carly's turn to feel—and no doubt look—poleaxed.

"O…kay," she said, feeling rebuffed. Adam could be positively blunt at times, and although she was aware of his abrupt manner, it still hurt. Why, Carly couldn't say, but after feeling so much a part of his family, she now sensed that Adam was trying to shut her out.

Angry with herself for caring so much and for letting her emotions show, she shrugged and laughed it off. "No hard feelings. Like I said, the other night was probably a mistake. I think we just got carried away with the moment."

Adam stared at her blankly, and she punched his shoulder lightly. "Lighten up, Adam." She winced inwardly as she said it.

He grunted and rubbed his shoulder. Without saying anything further, he strode toward the house, leaving Carly to wonder what he had to talk to his family about that was so important.

ADAM WAS GRATEFUL THAT Carly had offered to have all the children over at the apartment. What he had to tell the family wasn't fit for their ears. Cody was taking advantage of the school break to stay at a family friend's ranch for a few days.

Adam was stunned by his family's reaction to his confession about who was really driving Rory's car the day he died. The wailing he'd expected from his mom, the abject disappointment he'd expected from his dad, the loathing from his brothers and their wives—it didn't happen. None of them showed less than their complete compassion, support and forgiveness. They were so understanding that Adam suspected Matt might have prepared them for the news. But Matt was a man of his word. He'd have kept Adam's confession to himself, taken it to his grave.

Once Adam had answered their questions and assured them that he'd spoken to Jennifer Bennett, Matt said, "I'm glad we're all here. I have some worrying news."

"What is it, darling?" Sarah asked, her attention diverted from Adam for the first time that evening.

Matt stood and paced the living room floor. "Arson experts investigating the apartment building fire have discovered a link to Carly."

"Well, of course there's a link to Carly!" his mother burst out. "She *lived* there!"

"Mom, calm down," Matt said. "You're going to have to listen and let me finish. I don't want to believe what I've been told, but arson investigators and cops deal in facts, and the fact is, Carly's been linked to two previous fires."

"No!"

"Mom!"

"Sorry. Go on, dear. I'll try to control myself."

"As we all know, her husband died in a warehouse fire in San Diego."

When everyone nodded, he continued. "Her name was

also flagged in relation to the recent firebombing at the Colorado Grand Hotel. A few days after that, Carly moved to Spruce Lake. Then, just weeks later, the apartment building burned."

Silence descended on the room.

"You can talk now," Matt said into the silence. Then everyone started talking at once.

"That's complete B.S.!" Will said.

"I agree!" Sarah chimed in.

"This is surely just a coincidence?" Megan said.

"How unlucky can one person be?" asked Luke.

"You're saying that Carly is an arsonist and that she *deliberately* put her children's lives in danger?" Becky asked. "That's not possible. She adores those children."

Needing to put an end to any further speculation, Adam stood. "I'm going over there and I'm asking her about this."

Matt pushed him back down into his seat. "You'll do no such thing. Leave it to the officials to deal with any questioning."

"You can't think she's truly any threat," Sarah said. "Otherwise, you'd have arrested her...or something."

"The evidence is piling up, Mom. In a day or two they'll have their answer. I wanted to give you a heads-up."

"In the meantime, she's over there in that apartment, watching our kids," Luke pointed out.

Megan, Becky and Beth couldn't help jumping to their feet and racing to look out the living room window, toward the stables.

Chapter Eleven

Carly stared out the apartment window, down at the ranch house. All the O'Malleys had arrived nearly an hour ago. Carly had done as Adam requested and made herself and her children scarce. Luke's girls and Nick had wanted to come, too, and all eight children were now watching a DVD, although Charlie was dozing off, unable to stay awake past his usual bedtime.

As she filled a glass of water at the sink, Carly thought she spotted something in the yard below. A movement. Like someone snooping around. Hesistant to disturb Adam's meeting with his family, she decided to investigate it herself.

"Sash, would you and Nick mind keeping an eye on the kids while I take a walk?" she asked. "I won't be long."

"Sure," the girl said. "If we have any problems, I'll ring the fire bell."

Carly knew the stables had several fire bells installed, one of them in the apartment. "That's not a good idea. Someone might think there really is a fire."

"Nah, we use it for all sorts of things. Calling people for dinner and stuff. I'll only ring it if someone's really acting up or whatever. You go enjoy your walk."

Carly thanked her and pulled on her ski jacket, snow boots and gloves.

"Lock the door after me, would you, Sash?" she asked, then stepped outside and waited to hear the lock click into place.

A few minutes later, Carly went down the stairs and out the back door of the stables, hoping to come up behind whatever, or whoever, she'd seen moving in the yard.

She knew it couldn't be one of the ranch hands, since all three were in town celebrating Chuck's forty-ninth birthday. Beth had told her she didn't expect them back for hours. The large cabin they shared was annexed to the rear of the stables. The ranch dogs slept there, too. This evening the cabin was in darkness.

Carly walked farther across the yard, then froze in her tracks at the sight of a fox near the corrals. It stopped and gazed at her, then loped off into the darkness. She shook her head. That must've been what she'd seen from the apartment.

Since foxes didn't scare her, Carly took a moment to breathe in the crisp night air. She turned away from the ranch house, not wanting anyone inside to see her in case they thought she was spying. Not that any of the O'Malleys would think that. Only Adam. He was so closed off, so suspicious of everything!

As she trudged through the snow and out into the paddocks, a thought occurred to her. Why hadn't the ranch's dogs barked when the fox was in the yard? They usually went crazy if any wildlife was around. Luke had told her that bears often came into the area looking for food, but since the ranch had a strict policy about not leaving trash out, the bears soon moved on. However, this was winter and the bears were hibernating.

Before she had a chance to ponder the dogs' silence any further, the fire bell rang shrilly. Carly whirled around, ready to chastise Sasha for ringing the bell over some minor transgression by one of the younger kids.

What she saw turned her blood to ice. The stables were on fire!

She took off toward it, her feet barely touching the ground, her heart pounding with fear for the children inside.

Just as she made it to the rear stable doors, she saw the front door of the ranch opening and people pouring out.

She reached for the pull cord to turn on the stable lights, but nothing happened. Surely the electricity wouldn't have cut out this soon?

"Alex?" she screamed into the cavernous stables as she scrambled toward the apartment stairs. "Jake, Maddy! Where are you?"

The sound of her voice was drowned out by the screams of horses, terrified by the smoke that was filling the stables, and the sound of splintering wood.

She didn't have time to register where that was coming from. The stables were lit by a small battery-operated emergency light near the front entrance. Those doors, closest to the house, were usually left open until everyone had turned in. Only the rear doors were kept closed.

Carly got to the bottom of the stairs leading to the apartment at the same moment the children came tumbling down. "We're here!" Alex cried. "We're all okay!"

Carly hugged and kissed them all as Sasha brought up the rear, a sleepy Charlie in her arms. The same couldn't be said for Maddy and Celeste, who were alternately screaming and crying.

Carly threw an arm around each girl and followed Alex, Jake, Nick, Daisy and Sasha to the front of the stables.

The closed doors had been thrown open, and Adam

stood there framed in the moonlight, smoke billowing into his face. He held an ax. "Why the *hell* did you lock the doors?" he yelled, and then pushed past her.

"Get the children to the house," Luke said, charging in behind him, followed by his brothers. Carly could see Luke doing a head count of the kids. "Dad's called 9-1-1."

Shepherding the coughing children outside, she found Becky, Beth and Megan crossing the yard with Mac. "Come inside where it's safe, Carly," Megan said. "The fire department will be here shortly."

But Carly needed to stay and help. She passed the crying girls to Becky and Beth. Assured that all the children were in safe hands, she turned back to the stables.

"Where are you going?" Mac demanded. "Get in the house!"

Carly had never heard Adam's father raise his voice, but she didn't stop to contemplate his manner, or the strange way Megan was looking at her.

"I'll help get the horses out."

"The boys and I will do it," Mac said, but his command was lost in the sounds of whinnying horses as Matt and Jack led two of the terrified animals out of the stables, their heads covered with blankets.

Needing to feel useful, Carly reached for their bridles. "I'll take care of them," she said.

She turned and bumped into Mac.

"I'll take them," he said, and grabbed their halters.

Carly pivoted to see Will carrying one of the ranch dogs in his arms. "They've been doped, Pop," he said, and placed the dog on the snow-covered ground, out of the way of horses' hooves and any danger, if the stables collapsed.

Beth appeared and took the halters of two more horses

from Luke and led them toward the house, where Mac was tethering the first horses to the railing.

Adam was nowhere to be seen. Fearing he'd been caught in the fire, Carly plunged into the stables. Through the thick smoke, she could see him way in the back, hosing down the hay in the loft, while Jack was beating out flames. The hay blazed fiercely, sending sparks dancing up to the ceiling high above them and raining down on Adam and the horses still trapped in their boxes below.

Knowing there were at least a dozen horses still to be brought out, Carly wrapped her scarf over her nose. Her eyes burned as she opened the horse box closest to her. Finding it empty, she moved on.

She jumped as a horse kicked ferociously at the box she was passing. She glanced inside and recognized one of Luke's stallions. He'd warned her this one was ornery beyond belief. And now he was so terrified she could see the whites of his eyes through the gloom.

"Careful of him," Luke said, as he hurried by, taking two more of his precious mares to safety, followed by Matt leading their foals.

"There, boy," she murmured, carefully opening the door to his box and feeling along the wall for a rope to attach to his halter. The animal reared up in alarm. "I know, I'm scared, too," she said. "How about if you come with me?" she cooed, catching his halter and clipping the end of the rope onto it.

In the distance, above the sound of wood exploding and splintering as it burned, and the horses screaming in fear, Carly could hear sirens.

At last Adam would have more people to help him save the stables. But in the meantime, she had to save this horse. The only thing was, he wouldn't move! She tugged on the rope, but he backed up hard against the back of the box as if now that freedom was offered, he didn't want it.

"Damn it!" Carly growled. "Come on!"

She yanked the rope once more and the huge animal charged out of the stall, almost knocking her over. Carly recovered her footing before she hit the floor and held his rope more firmly. She closed the door behind her. Only yesterday, Daisy had been telling her that if horses were caught in a fire, they'd often run back to where they felt safe. Carly was thankful that she and Daisy had had that talk.

The headlights of the fire trucks were trained so they shone directly into the stables. Firefighters raced past her, armed with hoses and axes.

But the bright lights startled the stallion and he reared up. Carly stepped back, but not far enough or quickly enough. His front hoof glanced off her cheekbone and knocked her to the floor. Dazed, she lay there for a moment, recovering her breath.

The stables were suddenly silent, as if someone had hit the mute button during a very noisy action movie. She could see people rushing toward her, ready to help as the stallion reared up again. Determined to do this on her own, Carly staggered to her feet, clasped the halter in her left hand, pulled the stallion's head down and punched him in the nose. Shocked, he stopped tossing his head and stared down at her, nostrils flaring, hooves stamping the ground.

"Don't you ever do that again!" she roared, then wondered why she couldn't hear herself.

Luke grabbed the reins from her. His mouth was moving, but she couldn't hear him, either. She shook her head and yelled, "What?"

He gripped her elbow and led her and the horse out

of the stables. The cold, clean air made Carly gasp and cough. She tore the scarf away from her nose and coughed some more. She still couldn't hear herself.

"I think I'm deaf!" she shouted at Luke.

He nodded and passed her to his father, who led her and the stallion to the house. He tethered the horse to the veranda railing beside several others and turned toward her. His lips moved.

"What?"

He leaned closer and yelled in her ear, "I told you to go in the house!"

"No way! I couldn't leave those animals to die!"

He leaned toward her again. "You don't have to yell at *me*. I'm not deaf. You are!"

Carly blinked at him. "I am?" she asked. Almost involuntarily she raised her hand to the side of her head and hit herself, as if that would restore her hearing. Her hand came away covered in blood. "I'm bleeding," she muttered.

"And you've got a huge shiner developing under your eye."

"What?"

Mac shook his head, then led Carly up the veranda steps and handed her over to Sarah. He said something to his wife as he released Carly and hurried back to the stables.

"I have to help them," she said, but Sarah ignored her. Believing Sarah not to have heard her, she screamed, "I have to help them!"

Sarah grabbed Carly's hand when she tried to go back down the steps and held on tight. "Leave it to the men," she yelled into Carly's ear. "You're hurt. Come inside."

"I'm fine! I can help the dogs. Someone's doped them!"

She indicated Becky, collecting another dog from Will's arms and carrying it away from danger.

Carly was aware that she was shouting, but she wasn't sure how much Sarah could hear above the din that was coming from the stables and the railings where the horses were tethered, whinnying in fear. Daisy and Sasha were with them, trying to calm them down, soothing them with long, gentle strokes.

The ornery stallion was behaving himself, at least. Carly didn't know why she'd punched him like that; she'd only known she had to show him who was boss. She wanted to apologize to the horse, but she'd probably end up yelling at him and upsetting him more. Maybe when her hearing returned...

A paramedic approached her. She said something. Carly shook her head and pointed at her ears. "I can't hear!"

"You need to come inside so I can examine you!" she shouted into Carly's ear.

"Not until everyone's safe!"

She glanced back at the stables. The fire seemed to be under control. No more flames were visible, but smoke still poured from the doorway.

She saw the doped dogs lying in the snow and did a quick count. They were all there. Thank goodness Molly had stayed in the house! she thought. Still standing on the porch she saw Luke and Jack leading four horses from the rear of the stables, from the door she'd slipped out of earlier that night to investigate what she'd seen moving in the yard.

"That's the last of the horses, Grandma," Daisy yelled up to Sarah as she set off across the yard to help her father bring them in. "They're all okay!"

A couple of firefighters started picking up the dogs and

carrying them to the veranda. They were completely out of it, their tongues lolling out of their mouths, eyes unfocused.

Blankets were produced from the house and they were wrapped in them and taken inside to warm up.

Luke was attending to the horses, along with Matt and Mac. Will and Jack carried the remaining two dogs into the house.

Carly glanced toward the living room window and saw her children standing there, petrified. She waved to them to let them know she was fine. She should go to them and hold them and tell them yet again that everything was going to be all right. But they'd only worry more if she started yelling at them because she was half deaf. She'd give it a few minutes and then go see them.

Worried about Adam, she scanned the yard looking for him. He was the only one from his department who wasn't wearing protective firefighting gear. Was he okay?

She raced toward Matt. "Where's Adam? Is he out? Is he safe?"

He shook off her arm. "What do you care?" he shouted at her.

"What? What are you saying? I care a lot!" she screamed back, enraged by his attitude. "I haven't seen him since he first went in there!" Bewildered by his strange remark, Carly didn't immediately realize her hearing wasn't as bad as it had been minutes ago. She could actually hear herself. A little.

She dashed across the yard, counting the number of firefighters. There were two trucks, which meant eight firefighters. The battalion chief was there, too, but no sign of Adam.

"Where's Adam?" She grabbed the battalion chief's arm.

"Adam's in there?"

"Of course he is! He was using the fire hose in the stables!"

She released him and started for the stables, but the chief's arm shot out and held her back. "Let the men go in. It's too dangerous!"

"What?"

"Leave it to us!"

"No!" she cried, and broke out of his grip, running to where the smoke poured out the stable doors.

And then she saw him. He'd emerged from the damaged structure and was walking toward her.

She ran to him and threw her arms around his neck. "Oh, God! I thought you were dead!"

She felt rather than heard Adam's gruff laugh reverberate against her cheek.

He mumbled something, but she couldn't hear him. "You'll have to yell, I'm deaf!"

He smiled and nodded. His lips moved. Those lips she loved. "I love you!" she cried, and hugged him tighter.

Suddenly they were surrounded by children and adults and firefighters, and there was no chance to kiss Adam or talk anymore.

FINALLY, CARLY RELEASED her grip on Adam. He began to embrace Carly again, but Charlie was clinging to his leg. He hoisted the toddler into his arms and perched him on his hip.

Tears streaked down Charlie's cheeks and Adam wiped them away with a grubby finger. "It's okay, little guy. Everyone's fine."

Charlie still clung to him, his grip even fiercer than Carly's.

Adam turned to Carly and said, "I saw you hit the horse. That was brave."

"What?"

"I *said,* I saw you take charge of the stallion. That takes real guts."

Carly grinned at him. "I have no idea what you're saying," she yelled. "I'm deaf!"

"And so will we all be," said his mom. "If we don't get her checked out by the paramedics."

The group moved toward the house but Adam stayed where he was. "I need to invite my buddies in when they've finished up here," he told his mother.

"Already done, darling," she said. "Megan's making coffee and sandwiches as we speak and we'll be taking them to the guys who have to stay out in the cold to investigate the cause of the fire."

Adam didn't miss Matt and his father exchanging a glance. Surely they didn't think Carly was responsible for this fire, too? Or *any* fire!

He'd deal with the suspicions Matt had raised earlier in the evening, but not yet. For now, they all needed to get inside and warm. Although one thing kept playing on his mind: Who had locked the stable door? He'd had to break it down with an ax.

Once inside, Charlie allowed his mother to pry him away from Adam's neck and take him into the kitchen, which was full to overflowing with dogs, people and children. Carly's kids were mute with fear. He went over to them and sat down at the table. Maddy climbed up on his lap, shaking uncontrollably. He hugged her and spoke soothingly. Carly joined them holding Charlie, who had his thumb in his mouth and a soft toy clutched in his hand. She reached out to touch the back of Jake's head and draw him against her.

Carly's children seemed to relax a little once their mom was with them, but they'd been traumatized by the fire.

His nieces, however, seemed to think it was all a big adventure—apart from Celeste, who was holding on tightly to Luke. Daisy was happily looking after the horses outside, trading shifts with her father and grandfather to check on them.

Adam noticed Molly curled up on his old blanket. She was obviously confused, frightened by all the commotion. He indicated to Alex and Jake that they should go and comfort her. Both sat on the floor with her; Alex lifted her head into his lap while Jake rubbed her back. As the other dogs started to come to, Jake went to comfort them.

The boys had inherited their mother's healing touch, Adam decided, as each of the dogs gradually regained consciousness and moved to the sheltering warmth provided by the two boys.

Luke unwound Celeste's arms from his neck and gave her to Megan. The child went willingly, clinging to her stepmother.

"Once everything's settled down in the yard," Luke said, "we'll take the machinery out of the shed and set up temporary stables in there for the horses. The dogs will spend the night in the kitchen. First thing in the morning, I'll rent a couple of mobile homes for the ranch hands. I've already called Chuck and told them to stay in town for the night."

He turned to Sasha. "I'm so proud of you, honey, for handling everything so calmly when you noticed the fire and rang the alarm bell and got all the children downstairs safely." He glanced at his nephew. "You, too, Nick. I know you gave the credit to Sash, but you're equally responsible."

He kissed the top of his daughter's head and shook Nick's hand as the teenagers beamed with pleasure. Then he hurried back out to the yard, followed by Cody, Matt and Will.

Adam chugged down the glass of water his mother had given him and wondered yet again why those stable doors had been locked from the inside and where Carly was when it all started.

He leaned toward her and said, "I need to talk to you."

"What?"

Since she was still suffering the effects of being kicked in the head by the stallion, Adam decided their talk could wait until Carly completely regained her hearing.

Sarah clapped her hands, attracting their attention and stopping any further conversation. "We need to rearrange the sleeping around here. Sash is going home with Becky and Will. You can have her room, Carly, if that's all right with you."

Carly looked at her blankly. Adam knew his mother would sort everything out, and make sure everyone was happy, whether Carly could hear her or not. "Carly can have Sash's room and share it with Charlie. We have a portable crib up in the attic that Adam will bring down for him. And there are a couple of spare mattresses up there that Matt and Jack can get for the boys and put in Sash's room. Maddy can share with Celeste…"

This brought screams of excitement from the two little girls, who jumped to their feet, clapped their hands and raced upstairs without further encouragement.

"Since Daisy insists on helping out with the horses, she'll sleep on the sofa so she can be closer to them during the night. Okay, battle stations!"

Sarah clapped her hands once more and everyone sprang into action. In spite of the circumstances, Adam couldn't help smiling. His mom liked nothing better than organizing people. To her, this was like a military campaign.

He doubted that in the light of morning, when the damage to the stables was finally revealed, she'd be quite so chirpy.

"What's happening?" Carly yelled in his ear.

"Mom's rearranging sleeping quarters, and the paramedics are going to take a look at you."

They did and insisted on driving Carly to the E.R. for a scan to rule out a cerebral hematoma or any other injury, but she refused to go until Charlie was asleep and the boys and Maddy were tucked in.

Adam had dismissed the paramedics, saying he'd make sure she got to the E.R.

But now Adam could feel his frustration levels rising as she kissed each of her children good-night and patted Charlie's bottom until he'd drifted off.

Megan had said she wouldn't be able to sleep for the rest of the night with Luke reorganizing the stabling of the horses and having to keep up an endless supply of warm drinks for the workers. She'd stay in Sasha's room and keep an eye on Charlie and the boys until Carly's return.

Finally, Carly decided she was ready to leave. Adam helped her into his SUV and headed for the gates leading out of Two Elk Ranch.

As they crossed the cattle grid, he turned to face her and said, "Matt thinks you're an arsonist."

Chapter Twelve

"What?"

Adam realized she wasn't questioning his statement; she still couldn't hear properly. Carly also looked sleepy. The paramedics had been wary of leaving her behind, saying if she had a concussion, they should take her to the hospital immediately. But Carly was having nothing of it. Now Adam regretted not being more insistent that she drop everything and go straight to the hospital with them.

Was he supposed to keep her awake? "Carly? *Carly!*"

"Huh?" She snapped into wakefulness. "What's wrong?"

"You were falling asleep."

She frowned.

"Stay awake!" he yelled, and went back to concentrating on the road. He wanted to floor it, but that might jostle Carly too much and cause her more injury. He wanted her awake and alert when he asked her about those locked doors. Meanwhile, he tried to make the ride into the hospital in Silver Springs as smooth as possible.

I love you. Carly's words echoed in his mind. Had she meant them?

He'd sure liked hearing her say those three little words.

But then again, if she was suffering from concussion, she probably had no idea what she was saying.

AT THE HOSPITAL, CARLY was given a battery of tests and scans, then kept overnight for observation. Adam hadn't wanted to leave her, but he needed to get back to the ranch, to help clean up and restable the horses.

"HEY, MATT," CARLY greeted him the following morning as he entered her hospital room. "Is everything all right at the ranch?"

An uneasy feeling crept up the back of her neck. Matt wasn't smiling.

The uneasiness turned into a heavy sense of alarm, settling deep in her stomach. Sarah had sounded a little strange when Carly called the ranch earlier to check that her children were fine and to say that she expected to be discharged in the next hour or so.

"Everyone's safe," he said, his voice abrupt.

"Then why the frown?" she asked, needing to clear the air.

"I don't want to have to do this," he said, "but here goes. Carly Spencer, I'm arresting you on the charge of arson in the first degree."

"What?" Carly's hearing had been gradually returning, but now she wasn't so sure of that. "What did you just say, Matt?"

"You have the right to remain silent," he said. "You have the ri—"

"Is this some kind of a joke?"

"You have the right to an attorney."

"What?"

This time the query came from Adam. Carly had been

so transfixed by Matt's statement, she hadn't even noticed him entering the room.

Matt took a deep breath. "I'm sorry, Adam, but I'm arresting Carly for suspected arson. Four counts."

"Oh, come on!"

Matt turned back to Carly, all business. He looked so forbidding, she felt sick to her stomach. This couldn't be happening!

"I don't want to embarrass you by having to handcuff you, Carly. Will you come quietly?"

"No, she won't!"

"Adam, stay out of this and let me do my job," Matt growled. "Carly—"

But she was already climbing out of the bed and racing for the bathroom, wishing she hadn't eaten breakfast that morning.

She stumbled into the room, gripped the sides of the hand basin and threw up. The spasms seemed to last forever as her stomach surrendered its contents, and tears sprang to her eyes. Mortified, she ran water into the basin, then reached blindly for a towel.

One was placed in her hand, and a damp cloth was applied to the back of her neck, settling her churning stomach and taking away the urge to be sick again.

"It's okay," she heard Adam's soothing voice above the sound of the running water. "Hold on to me if you feel faint."

Carly wanted to weep at his kindness.

He turned her gently toward him and wiped her face with another damp cloth.

"Rinse out your mouth and I'll help you back to the room," he told her.

Confused, grateful, Carly obeyed, splashing water over her face and using the towel Adam had handed her to dry herself. She must look a mess—she sure felt like one—but Adam's dark eyes bored into hers, reassuring her and giving her the strength to return to the room where Matt waited to arrest her.

Arson?

Still shaky, she clutched Adam's arm as he helped her into the chair beside the bed. He stood beside her, a reassuring hand on her shoulder.

"Is she okay?" Matt asked his brother, as if she were incapable of speaking for herself.

"I'm…" She cleared her throat. "I'm fine," Carly said, gripping the arms of the chair. "But why on earth would you think *I* set that fire last night? My children were inside the apartment!" Her voice was shrill, but Carly didn't care. Now that she felt better, she was getting downright mad at Matt and his ridiculous accusation.

Matt took a seat in the other chair. "There are a number of reasons, Carly. First and foremost, you'd locked the stable door, preventing any of us from getting in to save the children and the horses."

Enraged, Carly sprang to her feet. "Kill my children! Are you *insane?* I didn't go *near* that door! What gives you such a stupid idea?"

Matt didn't flinch beneath her fury. "Sasha said you went out for a walk about ten minutes before the fire started."

Feeling light-headed, she resumed her seat. "That's correct. So?"

"You were the only person outside at the time. The rest of us were inside the house, talking to Adam. The kids were all upstairs in the apartment watching television. The ranch hands were in town for the night."

"Matt, that doesn't even make sense," Adam said. "What evidence do you have that Carly set the fire?"

"At present, it's mostly circumstantial. But in the past two years, Carly has been present at, or involved in, four sites that were the targets of arson attacks."

"What about the dogs?" Adam asked. "You think *Carly* drugged them?"

Matt sighed. "I don't know yet." He paused. "I was starting to explain to you all last night that the sheriff's department's been investigating the fire in the apartment building."

He turned to Carly to explain. "We have a national database into which we insert the names of fire victims and cross-reference links to other fires. It's mostly set up to deal with insurance fraud, but in this instance, it flagged you on three occasions, Carly." He glanced back at his brother. "Now four. However, I didn't get to finish what I was saying last night because the stable bell started ringing and we all ran outside to find it on fire."

Numb with shock, Carly could only sit there and listen to Matt. It was true; fire seemed to follow her everywhere.

Matt counted them off on his fingers. "The warehouse fire in San Diego that killed her husband. The firebombing of the Colorado Grand Hotel in Denver the night before it was due to open—"

"What the hell's that got to do with Carly?"

Carly finally found her voice. "I was about to start work in their spa."

Adam scowled at his brother. "Oh, come on, Matt! That's got to be a coincidence."

"Then there was the apartment building in town," Matt went on relentlessly. "Last night it was the stables. Next time it could be the ranch house."

"No! How can you think I'd do such a thing? How can you even *think* I'd hurt my children or anyone else?"

Matt shrugged, not meeting her eyes. "I don't know,

Carly. We're also going to request a psychiatric assessment."

"What the hell for?" Adam and Carly spoke at once.

For the first time since he'd walked into the room, Carly detected compassion in Matt's eyes. "Because the court's going to ask why a mother would put her children at mortal risk."

"But I didn't!"

"I don't know anything much about psychiatric illnesses, Carly. Maybe you have some form of Munchausen's syndrome by proxy?"

Carly shook her head. "I feel as if I'm trapped in some sort of terrible dream that I'm hoping to wake up from. But I suspect I'm already awake and this nightmare *is* my life."

She got to her feet and said, "The sooner you arrest me and take me in for questioning, Matt, the better. I want to clear my name and help find the real arsonist."

"Admirable, but you won't be helping us do anything, Carly. You'll be behind bars."

"I have children! I can't stay in jail! Who'll look after them?"

"Arson is a very serious offence. The D.A. will be asking the judge for a very large bail amount."

Carly slumped back in the chair. "Bail?" she muttered, staring at the floor. "I don't have a cent to spare." She stared up at Matt. "I realize you're doing your job, Matt. But do *you* honestly think I'm an arsonist?"

Matt took his time answering. "I hope not, Carly. I want to believe you aren't, but we're talking about people's lives here. Every time there's been a fire, you haven't had a viable alibi."

"Oh, Matt." Carly couldn't restrain the disappointment in her voice. In the short while she'd known him, she'd gauged Matt to be rock-steady, not the type of person to believe in hearsay and coincidence. "What alibis?"

"You claimed you were out shopping when the warehouse in San Diego went up. Yet you couldn't produce any receipts when asked."

"I didn't *claim* anything! I *was* shopping!"

"Let me finish please, Carly," Matt said. "You left your children with a sitter at your home in Denver and went out. During your absence, the hotel was firebombed.

"You told investigators you were working at the day spa in Spruce Lake the day of the fire in the apartment building, yet records show you'd left there nearly an hour earlier."

Carly opened her mouth to explain she'd gone grocery shopping, but Matt held up his hand.

"And last night, you conveniently went for a walk ten minutes before the fire broke out."

Carly's lips thinned. To think she'd liked Matt once upon a time. Now he was sounding like some sort of crazed, redneck law enforcer, ready to round up a posse and hang her from the highest tree!

"First, when Michael's superintendent told me about the warehouse fire and…and that he was missing, I dropped everything and drove like a maniac to the scene of the fire." She could feel her voice breaking at the memory. "So of course I didn't have any sales receipts! Neither did I have the items I bought. They were *dropped* somewhere on the streets of San Diego. Check your records.

"Three days after the fire and my husband's *death*—" she paused to let him absorb that "—I was questioned by the authorities as to my whereabouts at the time of the fire. It was only then that I realized I didn't have my wallet. Or my shopping. I'd driven straight to the scene, was told my husband had died and I collapsed. I was a basketcase for days afterward. People were coming and going, taking care of me and my children, so I hadn't needed to buy any food, or anything else for that matter. Once I realized what I'd done, I reported my credit cards missing and applied for another driver's license, ID and so on." She looked at him pointedly. "There'll be proof of that in the official records."

Matt nodded, but Carly wasn't sure he entirely believed her. "I was seven months pregnant, Matt. I was in so much shock, I nearly lost Charlie. The last thing I was worried about was some dumb shopping!"

Adam squeezed her shoulder and she reached for his hand, needing his touch. She smiled up at him, but Adam was glaring so hard at his brother, he missed it.

Carly returned her attention to Matt, determined to clear her name. "Second, yes, I'd left the children with a sitter while I went out to purchase some supplies in Denver. I'd be working during my older children's school hours and wanted to make up some dinners to freeze, so I'd have time to help them with their homework when they got home."

That sounded pretty thin even to her ears, yet it was exactly what she'd done.

"You moved to Spruce Lake within days of the Denver fire."

"Yes! I needed a job, since I no longer had one in Denver. The owner of the building I was living in offered me an apartment in Spruce Lake at a discounted rate, since it was slated to be demolished next summer. I wanted to get away from the city, start over in a small town, someplace where people cared about one another. I found a part-time job at the day spa, and I liked living in that apartment building. The rent was affordable, the neighbors were wonderful. I love Spruce Lake and thought I had a future here. Why would I jeopardize such an opportunity by setting fire to my home?"

"That's one of the things we're hoping the psych evaluation will tell us."

Too angry to protest, Carly could only close her eyes and shake her head. Eventually, she felt strong enough to open her eyes again and say, "I'll come quietly, Matt. But please, no handcuffs."

Chapter Thirteen

"I saw something moving outside and went to investigate," Carly said.

Matt exchanged a look with Adam.

They were sitting in the interrogation room at the sheriff's department in Spruce Lake. Carly's lawyer, Mike Cochrane, was present, as was Adam—at her request.

"I was hardly going to alarm the kids and say I thought there was a prowler in the yard, was I?"

"And was there?"

"No, it turned out to be a fox."

"What did you do then?"

"I walked away across the paddocks that are closest to the stables."

"We found your footprints in the snow," Matt confirmed.

"Then did you find the footprints of whoever set the fire?" Carly asked, hopeful.

Matt shook his head. "The snow around the stables was trampled. People have been walking all around that area, and it was impossible to distinguish one footprint from another."

"Just my luck," Carly muttered.

"So you walked away from the stables?"

"Yes, I slipped out the rear door, because I didn't want any of you seeing me from the house."

Matt's eyes narrowed in suspicion. She held up her hand. "I didn't want you seeing me and thinking I was snooping around, trying to listen in on the meeting Adam had called with his family. He'd made it seem so personal and acted pretty abrupt when he asked me to make myself scarce earlier in the day."

"I'm sorry, Carly," Adam said. "I hadn't meant to sound like that when I talked to you, but I had a lot on my mind. I needed to confess something very personal to them first."

"First?"

"I was going to tell you afterward."

"You're talking in riddles, Adam. Tell me *what?*"

"He'll tell you later," Matt interrupted. "Right now we need to get this interrogation over and done with."

Carly dragged her eyes from Adam. "Okay, then let's get it *over and done with,* so I can get back to my kids," she snapped. She rarely snapped at anyone, but this farce had gone on long enough. "I had Sasha lock the apartment door from inside. Then I went out the back door of the stables. I left it unlatched so I could get back in that way. At no time did I lock the front stable doors."

Matt nodded. "Go on."

"I noticed the fox, realized that must've been what I'd seen, so I walked a little farther into the paddocks to get some fresh air."

"There was a fox around and you kept on walking— away from the protection of the buildings?" Matt asked, incredulity dripping from his voice.

"I'm not afraid of foxes," she said, squaring her shoulders. "And I'm pretty sure if there'd been a wolf pack nearby, I would've heard them."

"That's risky thinking," Matt pointed out.

"I wasn't intending to go far and, like I said, I wanted to get some fresh air," Carly stated. It had been the secretive way the creature had moved that had caused her to investigate. Then she'd seen the fox and, knowing they move stealthily, she'd stopped worrying about a potential prowler.

She decided it was pointless to explain that to Matt again. "I was about to turn back when I heard the bell ringing," she continued. "I saw that the stables were on fire and ran like hell. The horses were going crazy in their stalls, but right then I just wanted to get to my kids. Luckily Sasha and Nick had collected everyone and started downstairs. I met them at the bottom of the staircase."

She glanced at Adam. "It was about then that I heard someone breaking down the front stable doors." She paused. "I'd heard the noise when I first entered, but as I said, the only thing I focused on was getting to my children. Later I discovered that the sound of splintering wood was Adam breaking down the door with an ax."

She paused again. "I remember something else."

Everyone in the room leaned forward.

"Yes?" Matt prompted when she didn't elaborate.

Carly held up her hand. "I'm trying to remember exactly when I realized this. Give me a few seconds." She ran through the events of the evening, starting with the moment she'd first walked outside.

"I was in the paddock walking away from the house, when I realized the dogs weren't barking and hadn't barked while the fox was around. I know they do that when strangers or wildlife are close by because Megan warned me about it."

She glanced over at Adam. "That's the reason I turned

back to the stables. I knew something was wrong. It was at that same moment that the bell began to ring."

"But someone doped the dogs," Adam said.

Carly nodded and turned to Matt. "But how did he get to the dogs to dope them in the first place without the dogs kicking up a fuss? I heard nothing while I was upstairs."

"Because whoever doped them was probably familiar to them," he said.

"And you're assuming that was me?"

He shrugged. "Like I said, the ranch hands were in town, the rest of us were in the house. You were the only adult not accounted for."

"Do you know how *stupid* and downright *irrational* that sounds?" Adam demanded of his brother.

"I can only go with the evidence."

"Yes, all of it circumstantial!" Adam sprang to his feet and grabbed Carly's hand. "Did it occur to you that it would be easy to dope a dog if you offered it a steak? The dogs were barking earlier, then they quieted. None of us went out to investigate!"

"He's got a point, Matt," Mike Cochrane said. "It wouldn't be hard to coax a dog with some meat. They'd swallow it whole."

"Let's get out of here," Adam said, pulling Carly to her feet.

Startled, Carly complied. She'd never had a truer champion. And right now, she'd rather be anywhere than here. Right now, she'd go wherever Adam wanted.

"Sit down!" Matt growled.

Carly glanced at Mike Cochrane and he nodded. Reluctantly, she resumed her seat. Even more reluctantly, she withdrew her hand from Adam's grasp.

"Adam, I'd like you to leave the room," Matt said, his voice low and threatening. "You're confusing Carly and clouding the severity of the matter. She's been charged with arson. In a few minutes we're going over to the courthouse where the D.A. is waiting to arraign her. Unless Carly can raise a substantial amount of bail, she'll be going to jail indefinitely."

"I haven't got any money for bail!"

"Then your children will be placed with protective services until your trial da—"

"No!" Carly cut him off. "How can you be so *inhuman?"* she demanded as tears filled her eyes.

Carly felt close to the breaking point. The past year and a half, after Michael's death, had been a living hell. The fight for the insurance payout, the decision to move from San Diego to get away from the unwanted attentions of Jerry Ryan and the peripatetic lifestyle she'd been forced to live since then—everything was all piling up, drowning her. And now to be falsely accused of arson?

"Believe me, Carly, I'm not trying to be, but I have to remain impartial. This is how we treat people who commit a serious crime and who can't pay the bail."

"I'll sell my house in San Diego!"

"I'm sorry, Carly, but posting a property bond is rarely done. So until you can sell your house, or post a bond through a bail agent—which, by the way, will cost you a minimum of ten percent of bail and in this case, it could be around fifty thousand dollars—you'll be in jail. And your children will be taken from you."

"Dammit, Matt!" Adam sprang to his feet and grabbed his brother by the collar, his right arm raised to punch him.

Matt refused to stand, refused to react to his brother's challenge. He sat there immovable, staring at Carly.

Adam eventually released him and paced the room. "What if I can raise the bail?" Adam said.

"Can you?"

"I don't know. How much would it be?"

"A lot more than you have. Probably more than you can borrow from a bondsman."

Adam sat down again and caught Carly's hand. "Whatever the outcome, I *won't* let them take away your kids and put them in a stranger's home."

Carly wanted to kiss him. But Matt's next words left her cold.

"I'm afraid you can't prevent any of this, Adam."

"I can, if I take her kids."

Three pairs of eyes turned in his direction. Mike shook his head, Matt snorted with derision and Carly gasped with relief.

"No can do. You're not registered with the department. And the security checks and hoops you'd have to jump through to get approval would take longer than her trial," Matt said.

ADAM TURNED TO MIKE for confirmation that what his brother stated was true. His shoulders fell when the attorney nodded.

Carly was sobbing and it was breaking Adam's heart. Okay, so he had no experience with kids, but neither did most men before they became fathers.

Carly's kids didn't deserve this. They'd been devastated when they lost their dad. Their lives had been turned upside down with too many moves these past few months. And they'd been completely traumatized by being caught in the middle of two fires. The one constant they'd been able to rely on was their mom. And now she was going to be taken away from them. He couldn't let her kids be thrown into foster care. Who knew what might happen to them? He guessed they probably wouldn't be placed in the same home. He also knew it could be months, maybe a year, before Carly's case came to court.

He couldn't imagine the trauma it would cause the children to be separated from one another and from their mother for that length of time. There was only one way to stop it.

"They won't be going to live with any stranger," he said to Matt, "because they'll be coming home with me."

"And I told you that can't happen."

"It can if I'm their father."

"What?" Carly, Matt and Mike demanded at once.

Adam turned to Carly, realizing he hadn't asked her what she thought of all this, but the tears in her eyes gave him the determination to go through with it.

Still holding Carly's hand, he stood abruptly, then bent a knee to touch the floor. "Carly, will you marry me?" he asked.

Chapter Fourteen

Silence filled the room.

Carly even managed to stop sobbing, but before she could answer him, Matt roared, *"Are you completely crazy?"*

Matt stood abruptly, launching into a tirade as he paced the room. "Carly's been involved in four fires in the past eighteen months, Adam. *She is going to jail.* Even if she somehow gets off, do you want a suspected arsonist living with you? Risking your life? Your home? Your family's lives?"

"That's enough!" Adam roared back at his brother, and stood, too. He kept Carly's hand firmly clasped in his.

"Carly is innocent. I'm convinced of it and I don't want to hear any more about this from you, of all people!"

Adam paused for a heartbeat, needing to get his temper under control. Unfortunately, that gave Matt the chance to further state his protests to Adam's marrying Carly.

"Adam, you're thinking with the wrong part of your anatomy. You're in lust, in thrall, in love, whatever! But you are *not* thinking straight. You can't marry Carly to save her. You can't marry her to stop her kids from being taken away. You can't marry her—"

"Excuse me?" Carly said, getting their attention. They stopped staring at each other and were now staring at her.

"Since this involves me more than it does you, Matt. I'd like to say something."

Matt nodded brusquely. Adam was so riled up, he couldn't wait to get Matt back at the ranch and give him the bloodiest nose he'd ever had.

"CONTRARY TO WHAT YOU might both think, I do have a brain and it functions independently of yours. So please don't talk about me as if I'm not here."

Carly waited while both men took that in.

She released Adam's hand and looked directly into his eyes. "Adam, thank you for the proposal. I appreciate it very much and I understand why you're doing it. I'm indebted to you for caring so much about my children that you'd make such an offer."

She turned to Matt. "I'm going to accept your brother's proposal and there's not a thing on God's green earth or in the state of Colorado that can stop me. I will do *anything* to ensure my children's safety and if that means marrying a man who doesn't love me, then I will."

"Who said I don't love you?" Adam asked.

"You've never said you do," Carly told him.

"I…I," Adam started to say, but Carly shook her head.

"It's okay, Adam. We hardly know each other. Once all this is over, we can get a divorce, move on with our lives."

"Thank you," Adam said with a smile that made her love him even more. "But what if I don't want a divorce?"

Carly's heart overflowed with something for this man, but was it love? Or gratitude? "You? One of Spruce Lake's most eligible bachelors, with a wife and four children? I don't think so."

"You got that right," Matt muttered.

Adam took a step toward his brother but Carly placed

a hand on his chest. "Let's not add 'assaulting an officer of the law' to the mix. It could affect your custody of my children."

"You'd grant him custody of your kids?" her attorney asked.

"Of course I would. I trust Adam implicitly. He's proven himself to me time and time again, starting with the day he saved my son from the apartment fire. I can't see the court denying custody to a hometown hero."

Adam coughed, bringing her attention back to him.

"About that. We need to talk," he said.

AT ADAM'S REQUEST, MATT had granted him the use of his office, posting a deputy outside the door.

Adam paced the room, not sure where to begin. Finally, he stood facing Carly, who'd sat on Matt's sofa. "I've been carrying something around with me for a very long time. It's affected my life, my relationships, everything."

"Does it have anything to do with your reaction to the massage I gave you the other day?" Carly asked.

"Everything," he said, and pulled up a chair in front of her.

"When I was fifteen, my best friend, Rory Bennett, and I went for a joyride. Rory stole a pickup truck and I drove it. Being fifteen I was full of bravado and showing off. I took a corner too fast and smashed into a tree. Neither of us was wearing a seat belt. I got thrown through the window. Rory was scrabbling around on the floor trying to find a CD he'd dropped. He was jammed in the cab, crushed to death."

"Oh, Adam," Carly said, and clasped his hands.

He bowed his head. "Please, let me finish."

"Of course."

Adam looked up; he could read the compassion in her eyes and loved her for it.

"I was in a coma for nearly a week. When I came out of it, Rory's funeral had already taken place. Because of the position of his body in the cabin of the truck, the cops concluded he'd been driving. I was a scared, stupid, cowardly fifteen-year-old and I never said a word."

"But why? Surely you were too young to be arrested?"

"I don't know about that. But my big brother was with the sheriff's department. He had his career all mapped out. How would it look if his brother was arrested for vehicular homicide? How would it affect my family, to know I'd killed my best friend? So I kept quiet."

Carly lifted her hand to his cheek. "And you've been carrying around this guilt for all these years?"

Adam leaned into her palm, needing the closeness, needing her warmth and reassurance. He wasn't sure what love felt like, but for the first time, he'd met a woman he didn't want to be parted from. A woman he wanted to spend the rest of his life with.

"I suspected you'd been holding something in that day I gave you a head massage. In fact, I suspected it when I gave you a massage in the apartment over the stables. I touched a trigger point and you flinched. I backed off. I didn't want to bring back bad memories when you were so vulnerable."

He turned his face into her palm and planted a kiss there. "You can genuinely tell that someone's holding in some deep hurt simply by massaging them?"

She nodded. "I can also help you heal."

Adam wanted to weep. He wanted so much to be healed of the guilt, to be forgiven, to be able to forgive himself.

He drew Carly into his arms.

She went willingly, surprising him as she wound her

arms around his neck. He brought her closer, needing her more than he needed air.

When they both pulled back from the kiss, Carly's face was wet with tears.

Raising one hand, he traced a tear down her cheek. "I love you," he whispered.

His confession triggered a fresh surge of tears from Carly.

She eventually got herself under control. "You don't have to say that just because you asked me to marry you."

He grinned. "I know. But I want to, because I mean it. I've shut myself off from so many people—from my family especially—for too many years. But now it's time for me to start living my life. It's time for me to let others in. Beginning with you."

Carly hugged him close. "Thank you," she said, smiling through her tears.

Some time later, a knock at the door interrupted them. And a good thing, too, Adam mused as he reluctantly lifted Carly off his lap and put her back on the sofa. He grabbed one of the cushions, set it in his lap and said, "Come in."

"Darling! What have you gone and done?" his mother asked.

Chapter Fifteen

Carly was surprised by how noisy the courtroom was when she entered it. Louella Farquar, the mayor's pet pig, was alternately screeching and snorting at the judge—none other than Becky O'Malley, Will's wife. Finally, Becky had had enough of the pig and the noise of the courtroom audience and banged her gavel.

"Mayor Farquar, you promised me that Louella had mended her ways since you married Mrs. Farquar and moved into town a year ago. However, this is the third complaint in as many weeks that the court has heard about her. Her recidivist behavior is unacceptable and antisocial. Either you restrain her from wandering about town on her own, causing havoc with traffic and tourists, or I'll find a permanent solution," she said.

Carly was standing so close to the judge's podium, she was sure she caught the words *bacon factory* muttered under Becky's breath.

"But, Judge, Louella doesn't like staying inside all day," the mayor protested.

"Louella is a *pig!* Why do I have to keep reminding you of that, Mayor Farquar? She doesn't belong inside all day, but she also doesn't belong downtown. I suspect half the reason you got yourself elected was in order to change the ordinance regarding the keeping of livestock within the town limits. Now, get her out of my court, and if I ever see her—or you—here again, I will personally run you *both* out of town!"

"You can't do that," he objected. "I'm the mayor!"

Becky peered over her glasses at him and said, "Try me." She banged her gavel, signaling the case was dismissed.

A whistle of approval sounded from the rear of the courtroom, almost drowning out the screeches of Louella as she was led off. "Way to go, darlin'," Will O'Malley cheered.

Becky's face looked like thunder. She obviously hadn't expected to see her husband in court. Nor the rest of his family, Carly noted as the courtroom filled with O'Malleys. How they'd gotten there so quickly, Carly couldn't imagine.

Becky picked up the file her clerk had placed in front of her and scanned it, then took off her glasses and gazed down at Carly.

She addressed the court. "Given the nature of the next case and the fact that I know the accused, I'm going to recuse myself."

A collective sigh of disappointment rose from the audience. This wasn't good. When Carly had learned that Becky was the judge she'd be appearing before, she was hoping she'd get off with a low bail, maybe none. But if Becky recused herself, Carly's situation became even more dire.

"As it's almost lunchtime, I'm calling a recess," Becky said.

"What's this mean?" Carly hissed at Mike.

"It means the court's adjourned until after lunch."

"I know that!" Carly rolled her eyes. "I mean if Becky recuses herself, when's my hearing?"

"It'll have to be postponed until tomorrow when Judge Stevens is in session."

"But I can't stay in jail overnight!"

Cochrane stepped forward and said, "Your Honor, my client has four young children to care for. It would be cruel to expect her to wait in jail until her arraignment, simply because you've chosen to recuse yourself."

"Simply?" Becky repeated. "There is nothing *simple* about this case, Mr. Cochrane. Your client has been charged with four counts of arson. I know her, therefore I cannot preside over this bail hearing."

"I understand that, Judge. But there are extenuating circumstances. Her children—"

His explanation was halted by the appearance of Judge Stevens, who entered the court and asked if she could approach the bench. Her request was granted, and as she walked to the front of the courtroom, Carly saw Matt slip in and nod at Adam.

The two judges conferred for several minutes and then Becky said, "Judge Stevens has offered to hear this bail application in my place. We can proceed immediately if that's all right with both the prosecution and the defense?"

The D.A. and Mike agreed, and Becky vacated her chair after saying, "In that case, I'll adjourn the court for ten minutes while my learned colleague familiarizes herself with the charges."

Carly wasn't sure whether to cheer or cry. At least she'd be able to go home to her children tonight—provided the bail wasn't too steep. Although looking at Judge Stevens, Carly suddenly wasn't feeling so confident.

CARLY'S WORST FEARS were realized when the D.A. presented a very convincing case and the judge set bail on four counts of arson at four hundred thousand dollars.

Carly collapsed and had to be helped from the courtroom by the bailiff and her attorney.

Adam ignored all propriety, jumping over the low barrier separating the courtroom from the audience. Carly was aware of the judge banging her gavel, but didn't know what Adam had done until he hoisted her into his arms and carried her into the area behind the courtrooms.

"It's okay. I can walk," she said. "Please put me down."

Reluctantly, Adam did, allowing her feet to touch the floor. He held on to her until he was sure she could stand by herself.

"I didn't mean to frighten you," she apologized to the three men present. "But that was worse than I expected."

The bailiff and Mike nodded. Mike said he'd see her later, then both of them departed.

Carly wrung her hands. "Where on earth will I get that kind of money?"

"I have savings," Adam said. "Nothing like that, of course, but a bit."

Carly shook her head. "Thank you, but I can't accept it. To be perfectly honest, Adam, I can't guarantee that if I get released on bail I won't grab my children and hightail it to Canada or South America. Or Tasmania."

"I didn't hear that," another voice said.

They spun around to discover Matt standing behind them.

Adam's eyes narrowed. "I *was* going to thank you for finding Judge Stevens and getting her to court to hear the bail application, but you'll understand why I won't."

"Adam, Carly got off lightly. The usual amount of bail for first-degree arson is considerably more."

"And that makes me feel so much better," Adam muttered.

"Listen, I'd help with the bail, but all Beth's and my

savings have gone into building the house. Likewise with Will and Becky."

"And believe me, we'd help if we could," Becky said. They turned to see her in a doorway behind them. Carly glanced at the office nameplate. Judge Rebecca O'Malley, it read.

Carly turned to Matt. "Do I get taken to jail now?"

"I'm afraid so," he said. "But since I'm here and it can be construed that you're in custody, we don't have to go back right away."

Matt looked up and down the corridor, then said to Becky, "Is it okay if we use your office for a while? I'd like us to meet with Mom and Pop and see what we can figure out."

Becky's face lit up. "Sure. I'll go find them. I'm not sure who's more trouble in court, Louella Farquar or a whole passel of O'Malleys."

She took off down the hallway in search of her in-laws. Matt pushed the door open and gestured that Carly should precede him into the room. Adam brought up the rear.

Adam was about to say something but Matt stopped him. He arranged three of the visitors' chairs into a small circle and indicated they should sit. Once they were all facing one another, he said, "I want to apologize to you, Carly, for having to arrest you, but I had no choice. I'm also sorry about how steep the bail is, but that's out of my control.

"What *isn't* out of my control is you two marrying right now, in order for Adam to have custody of your children." He turned to Adam. "Are you still of that mind?" he asked his brother.

"Of course," he said, reaching for Carly's hand.

"That's very sweet of you, Adam," she murmured. "But there are laws governing blood tests and waiting periods, aren't there? I could be in jail for weeks before we'd be eligible to marry."

Adam and Matt exchanged furtive smiles. "What are you two up to?" she demanded.

"I suspect," said Becky, coming through the door, followed by Adam's parents and the rest of his brothers, "that Matt hopes I'll waive the usual waiting period and marry you and Adam right here and now."

Carly's spirits lifted. "You can do that?"

"If I can run the mayor and his pig outta town, I can surely marry two people who are so obviously in love that there's no need to wait several weeks."

"Oh, that's wonderful!" Sarah O'Malley cried, and hugged her son. She smiled at Carly with tears in her eyes. "I'm so happy to welcome you to our family."

"I thought you hated me…"

"No! Never. Where on earth did you get that idea?"

"You acted strange on the phone this morning. I thought it had to do with me being suspected of burning down the stables with my children and your grandchildren inside."

"Not to mention the horses," said Luke.

"And the dogs," Will added.

"Then you really do believe I'm innocent?"

"Of course we do!" they all chorused.

"There's still the circumstantial evidence," Matt reminded them.

Luke grabbed Matt in a headlock and pretended to punch some sense into him. "Sometimes you take your job too seriously."

"He's a very serious person," said Beth, coming into the room. "What's up? Mac phoned and told us to get down here ASAP." She moved aside, so Megan could enter, too.

"Adam and Carly are getting married!" his mother said.

"So they've dropped the charges?" Megan said, and threw her arms around Carly in congratulation.

"Er, no," Adam told her. "But I'm marrying Carly so her children will be living with someone they know while she's in jail."

"Sorry, can you rewind all this? I'm totally confused." Megan patted her stomach and moved to her husband's side. "Pregnancy brain."

"Carly's bail is set at four hundred thousand dollars," Matt explained.

Soft whistles filled the room. "We could help out," Will said. "If we all pool our resources, we might be able to come up with something close to that. And if we can't, I'm sure Frank would come to the party."

"Not after this morning," his wife reminded him.

Frank Farquar was believed to be richer than Croesus. He was generous, but given that he was mayor of a town in which one of the fires had been set, he was unlikely to contribute to the cause. There was also the matter of Louella.

"I could offer to give him a lifetime of 'get out of court free' cards for Louella," Becky said.

"There's such a thing?"

"Of course there isn't." She smacked her husband good-humoredly. "But Frank doesn't know that."

Carly was enjoying the banter. It was what she loved about the O'Malleys, their ease with one another. But she didn't enjoy the thought of spending the night in jail, or however many nights after that. She couldn't put these people in debt to help her, though. Somehow she'd raise the bail. She'd start by selling her home in San Diego. It wasn't as if she wanted to return there anytime soon.

Ideas for raising bail money were flying around the room. Carly's head was spinning as she tried to sort one from the other. Finally, she put a stop to it by raising her hand and requesting silence.

With all eyes trained on her, she cleared her throat and said, "Thank you. All of you. You're wonderful people and I appreciate from the bottom of my heart your attempts to help me. But I have to be honest with you, if I'm released on bail, I *will* take my children and run."

There were gasps of shock, followed by a great deal of denying that Carly would do any such thing. They were finally silenced when Sarah declared, "And in your position, Carly, I'd do exactly the same thing."

"Mom!"

"Matt!" she said, mimicking him. "I would."

"And I'd go with her," Mac said.

"Well, that's a given," Will said with a smile, and dug his elbow into Luke's ribs.

"You'd run, even though you claim to be innocent?" Luke asked.

"I don't *claim* to be innocent, Luke. I am. And yes, I would, because if the case went against me, I'd lose everything that's dear to me. My only alternative is to run. I can't accept your money. But thank you all for offering."

She took a step toward Becky. "I'll be able to post bail once my home in San Diego is sold, but in the meantime, I'm resigned to going to jail. I'd very much appreciate it if you'd do Adam and me the honor of marrying us."

"Here?" Sarah cried.

"Yes, Mom, right here. Right now," Adam said. "Would you stand up for me?" he asked Jack, and all his brothers came forward.

Becky smiled and said, "We just need one of you. Now, Carly, who would you like to stand up for you?"

Carly looked at the other women in the room. "All of them. But since you're being economical…" She turned to Megan and said, "Would you be my matron of honor?"

Tears sprang to Megan's eyes and she hugged Carly.

"If all of you women don't stop crying, the wedding photo will be a mess." Will held up his camera phone.

"Glad that's settled," Becky said, giving her husband a warning glare. "Next, I need your IDs and birth certificates."

"All my papers were lost in the apartment fire. I haven't had time to replace them," Carly wailed.

"Don't upset yourself," Becky said, and sat at her computer terminal. After getting Carly's birth details, she tapped the information into the computer. Satisfied that Carly was who she said she was, she looked up at Adam, then his parents. "Do you solemnly swear that this man is your son?"

Mac and Sarah nodded enthusiastically. Mac even placed his hand over his heart.

"Carly and Adam, are you both sure this is what you want?" she said, glancing first at Adam and then at Carly, who both nodded.

"I have a distinct feeling of déjà vu," Megan murmured to her husband.

Carly turned to her in confusion.

Megan waved her concerns away. "Long story, tell you later," she said. "Hurry up and get married, you two, so we can start celebrating."

Unfortunately, her excitement fell flat as everyone realized that they couldn't have a celebration while the bride was in jail.

"I'm sorry, Carly. I wasn't thinking."

Carly gripped her hand. "We'll celebrate. But let's wait until I'm free and all the children are present."

Megan nodded. "I'll make sure it's extra special."

FIVE MINUTES LATER, there were hugs and handshakes all around. Carly detected a tear in Mac's eyes. More worrying was the look of desolation on her husband's face.

Her husband. Had she really done this? Married a man she barely knew? Carly stared down at her left hand, where Sarah O'Malley's wedding ring adorned her third finger.

"This has been a lucky ring," Sarah had said to Carly as she removed it from her finger and dropped it in Adam's hand. "I hope it'll help bring you both everlasting happiness, too."

Carly had been too choked up to reply. Adam had kissed his mother's cheek and whispered, "Thanks, Mom. I'm sure it will."

Was that just lip service, trying to reassure his mother that her ring would be lucky for them? What sort of future could they have with her in jail? They couldn't even plan a honeymoon! And soon, Carly would have to return the simple but beautiful band to its owner. She wouldn't be permitted to wear jewelry in jail.

"I think we should give these two some privacy," Matt said above the din of so many people talking at once. "I'll be waiting outside the door, so don't do anything inappropriate, okay?" he warned his brother.

"That sofa of Becky's—" Will started to say but was shushed by his wife and pushed toward the door. But Will wasn't done yet. "And don't forget the desk—"

He was cut off by the door's closing, leaving Adam and Carly alone at last.

He smiled down at her. "Are you a sofa or a desk kinda gal?" he teased.

She pretended to slap him in reproof. "If we knew each other better—the way a married couple should—you'd have the answer to that."

He rubbed his hands together. "I'm always up for some research."

"Adam, stop it!" Carly said, trying to keep a straight face. In a little while, they'd be separated for who knew how long.

"Thank you for trying to make me forget what lies beyond that door, but right now, I'm not in the mood for laughing. Or sex."

He drew her into his arms. "I know that, honey… Do you mind if I call you honey? Maybe you'd prefer darlin'? Sweetheart?"

"Carly will do. Please stop kidding around, Adam. I have a lot to tell you about the children and not much time."

Adam led her toward the sofa, sat and pulled her onto his lap. "Talk," he said, and nuzzled her neck.

"I can't concentrate when you do that!" she protested, loving every second of it.

"Okay, you have five minutes to talk and then we're going to do some serious necking."

Warmth flooded Carly. She might not know this man very well, but he was exactly what she needed. Exactly what her kids needed.

She rested her head against his chest and started speaking. "I'm instructing Mike Cochrane to make arrangements to put my San Diego house on the market."

Adam started to say something, but she silenced him with a finger placed over his lips.

"If you keep interrupting, there'll be less time for necking."

"Can you talk faster, then? I want to neck."

"Adam, this is important."

"Okay, but skip the changing diapers lesson. I already know how to do that. I also know how to cook nutritious meals."

That reminded Carly of something very important. "Hang on," she said, "Who's going to look after my children when you're at work?"

"Mom. Will. Megan. Beth. Everyone at the ranch will pitch in. Rory's mom, Jennifer Bennett, is watching them today. Mom's been in touch with her. I'd like you to meet her sometime."

"I'd like that," Carly said with a smile. She was happy Adam had reached out to Rory's mom.

"I promise you the kids will be perfectly safe and well cared for at all times, so please cross that off your list. Can we get to the good part about being married now?" He nuzzled her neck.

She snuggled against him and said, "I'm so scared, Adam. I've never been to jail before."

"You're afraid it'll be like on those reality TV shows?"

"Yes." The violence between the inmates depicted on those programs chilled her to the marrow.

Adam held her close. "Let me assure you, the county jail isn't like that."

"And you know this how?"

"I've been there."

"You've been in jail?"

"No, Matt took me on a tour when he became sheriff. You won't be with hard-core prisoners. Just druggies, drunks and illegal aliens."

"Oh, wow, can we skip the necking and go straight to jail in that case?"

Adam kissed her and she could feel his smile. He finally broke away and said, "Do you know when I first started falling in love with you?"

Carly could feel her heart blooming in her chest. This wasn't the conversation she'd expected they'd be having right now. "No, when?"

"When I coughed up all that black goop onto your white sneakers and you said, 'Thank you.' I liked the way you took it all in your stride."

"I wasn't thanking you for spitting on my shoes. I was thanking you for saving my son. And Molly."

"I know. But at the time, it intrigued me. It also scared me."

"Why?"

"Because you read me so well. You asked if I always deflected compliments. You're the only person who's ever asked me that. Ever noticed." He brushed a strand of hair out of her eyes. "I should've known then that you'd be trouble."

She punched Adam lightly and then kissed him.

When they came up for air, he asked, "Are we officially in necking time now?"

"Not yet. There's something important I want you to do for me."

"Consider it done."

"Can you phone my parents? Speak to my mom, not my father. He's recovering from a stroke and I don't want him to hear about this. If the news service gets hold of the story and it's broadcast nationally for some reason, my dad will hear and there's nothing I can do about it. I haven't even told them about the fire at the apartment building. They were so distraught after Michael's death,

I didn't want them to know how close their grandchildren came to dying."

Adam nodded solemnly.

"Now, since I'll be a guest of the county for the next days or weeks, however long we need to clear my name, I need to fill you in on what my children—"

"Let's take this one day at a time," Adam suggested. "When I think of next week and the possibility that you'll still be in jail, I feel physically ill."

"Try thinking about next month," she said grimly. "Next year."

"Why don't we concentrate on the present?" He reached for a notepad and pen from Becky's desk. "Write down your parents' details and I'll call your mom tonight. How's she going to take this?"

"Not well. But she's a strong woman. She's had a lot to deal with."

"Which highlights how little we know each other," Adam said, and regretted his words the moment he'd spoken. "Not that I'd take back marrying you," he hastened to say.

Carly touched his cheek. "I've had the same thought. I hope we can make up for lost time soon. Fill in the blanks about ourselves and our lives."

"Meanwhile, Matt will keep working to find the real arsonist." He paused and then said, "If you think of anything, Carly, no matter how insignificant you feel it is, tell him about it. He'll follow up on any lead."

"Believe me, I'll try. I haven't had time to think at all in the past week. Maybe it's a good thing I'll have time on my hands now."

"Was that supposed to be a joke?"

"A really bad one," she agreed. "I'll focus on why those fires happened when I was around." She glanced at the door. "In the meantime, can we forget about everything else for a few minutes? Except each other?"

Adam grinned, scooping her onto his lap. He pulled her close and they kissed as though it would be their last time.

Chapter Sixteen

Matt's soft knock at the door signaled that they'd soon be parted.

Reluctantly, Carly climbed off Adam's lap. He caught her hand and pulled her back down to sit on his knee. She slid her arms around his neck.

"Before you go," he said. "Tell me about that man you were kissing in the supermarket the other day."

"What is this? Belated jealousy?" Carly demanded, annoyed that Adam would bring up Jerry at a time like this. "For starters, I didn't kiss him, he kissed me. Couldn't you tell I wanted nothing to do with the guy?"

"He seemed pretty possessive of you."

Carly sighed and got up off Adam's knee. "Too possessive. He's the reason I left San Diego."

"Were you dating him there?"

Carly whirled around. "No! He was a colleague of Michael's. He helped me out after Michael died."

"What was he doing here in Spruce Lake?"

"I don't know. He claimed he was on vacation." Carly shrugged. "I got the shock of my life when he approached me in the supermarket. I couldn't wait to get out of there. Then you showed up and all I could think of was protecting you from him."

"Protecting *me?* Why?"

"Jerry's...obsessive. He's...scary."

"Why didn't you mention this to me?"

"I thought he was out of my life. I didn't tell him where I was moving because I didn't want him following me. Jerry got way too possessive of me and my time after Michael died. At first I assumed he was just being supportive, but then it got creepy. He was over at our house every night whenever he was off-duty, bringing food, asking me out to dinner. In the end, I decided to leave town."

"Did you tell him where you were going?"

"Of course not!"

"Is there any way this Jerry guy could know where you were planning to work in Denver?"

"He...could have. He and my mom were close," she said, then glanced at Adam. "It was the day after I told her I was about to start a job at the Colorado Grand that it was firebombed."

Adam nodded. "How do you think he found you in Spruce Lake?"

Carly hesitated, then continued, her face flushed. "I emailed my mom last week and told her I'd moved to Spruce Lake, that it didn't work out in Denver. I didn't tell her about the hotel being firebombed. She didn't need to worry about that."

Adam stood and paced the room. "Could he be obsessive enough to try to get you to return to San Diego by destroying the hotel—where you were about to start work?"

"Maybe..." Carly said slowly. "But I never made that connection because of all the media stories about how it had to be a Mafia hit or something."

"And if he knew you were in Spruce Lake..."

"Back up a bit. Are you saying *he* caused the fires in the apartment building and last night, as well? That's impossible! My children were in those buildings. He was devoted to them after Michael died!"

"Like he was *devoted* to you?" Adam said drily.

Confused, Carly searched her memory. Come to think of it, there'd been times when she'd wondered how genuinely Jerry cared for her kids. His devotion seemed a little overdone, as if he was trying to impress her.

Something else pricked at her memory.

"What's the matter?" Adam asked.

Carly explained the weird sensations she'd experienced—at the apartment fire, on the porch at the ranch and then the other day, just before Jerry had approached her in the supermarket.

"What if he *was* there on those occasions, Adam, watching me? What if he'd been there because *he'd* lit those fires? What if it was Jerry I saw lurking in the yard last night?"

There was another knock at the door, and Matt came into the room.

"I gave you both enough time to get yourselves decent," he said. "But—"

"Matt, can you check out a Jerry Ryan of San Diego?" Adam asked urgently. "He's a firefighter there."

"Whoa! What's this all about?"

As succinctly as he could, Adam detailed his discussion with Carly. "If you could check airplane records, rental cars in Denver, ascertain whether he stayed anywhere locally—anything that might link him to the fires—I think you'll find the real arsonist."

"IS THERE ANY OTHER way Jerry Ryan could've found out where you'd moved?"

"The only person in Denver who knew where I'd gone was the owner of the apartment I rented there…"

"And he owned the same apartment complex you moved to here in Spruce Lake," Matt finished for her.

"Yes," Carly said, but her voice was little more than a squeak. Had Jerry Ryan stalked her all the way to Denver and then Spruce Lake?

"You said this guy was obsessed with you?"

Carly nodded.

"Then it's possible he was burning those places down so you'd have nowhere to work or live and have to return to San Diego—and to him."

"Adam suggested the same thing. But is one person capable of that sort of evil?"

"Hell, just this morning, I was wondering if you were."

"Yeah, thanks so much for that."

"Carly, you have to know I was only doing my job. If I didn't arrest you, then someone else would have, and it might not have gone so well for you."

"Four hundred thousand dollars is *going well* for me?"

"Well, not that part. But look on the bright side. You got a husband out of it."

Carly gazed at him, deadpan.

"Sorry, bad joke."

"No, you're right, I did get a husband out of it, so the day wasn't a complete loss." She hugged Adam to her and kissed him soundly.

Matt strode toward the door. "I'm going to check Jerry Ryan's whereabouts on the relevant dates. Hopefully, we'll find the link we're looking for. But in the meantime, Carly, I'm afraid you're going to have to accompany me to jail."

Chapter Seventeen

As she'd expected, Carly didn't sleep. She tossed all night long, worrying about her kids. About Adam. Whether Matt would uncover a connection between Jerry and the fires.

She gave up on sleep shortly before dawn and lay on her bunk, hands clasped behind her head, and stared at the ceiling.

Adam was right; the jail wasn't so bad. It was new and clean and there were only two other female inmates, both illegal immigrants, on the women's side, so they each had a cell to themselves. Come the weekend—if she was still here—Carly suspected she'd be sharing with someone who'd been arrested on drug charges or for drunken behavior. She wasn't looking forward to that.

Sometime later, Carly heard a familiar voice in the corridor outside. Her cell door was unlocked and Matt stepped inside, followed by Adam. Adam smiled as he drew Carly into his embrace.

Matt's research had proven a direct link to the dates of the fires and the dates Jerry Ryan was in the vicinity. The owner of the apartment building in Denver had confirmed that a man matching Jerry's description had queried him about where Carly had moved. When he'd refused to tell

him, the man had gotten downright threatening. In the
end, the owner had threatened to call the cops. Jerry had
left him alone after that. It wasn't until Carly had emailed
her mom that he'd managed to track Carly to Spruce Lake.

"But surely this is as circumstantial as the evidence in
my case?" Carly said.

Matt shook his head. "Better than circumstantial. Jerry
was arrested by San Diego police as he got off a flight
from Denver this morning. He fell apart and confessed
to everything—including the fire at the warehouse where
your husband died." Matt gave a wry grin. "Must ask
them about their interrogation tactics sometime."

Carly breathed in the crisp mountain air as she walked
outside the county jail to be greeted by the O'Malleys. Her
children climbed all over her and she reveled in it. Charlie
perched on her hip and clasped her cheeks in his chubby
little fingers and kept kissing her.

"Is it true Adam's our daddy now?" Maddy asked.

Carly glanced up at him. Now that she was free, did he
want to stay married to her? she wondered.

Adam looked as uncertain as she felt.

"You can have it annulled, if you want," she whispered.

Adam frowned. "Do *you?*" he asked.

"I don't want you to feel trapped because you did something for me and my kids out of the kindness of your
heart."

"I *don't* feel trapped," he said, his voice rising. "I love
you, Carly."

"And that would be a *yes* to Maddy's question!" Will
shouted to the gathered crowd, and they cheered. "Come
on, you two, we're having a wedding breakfast at Rusty's.
I'm starving!"

Adam picked up Maddy, then turned and clasped

Carly's hand. "Ready to start the rest of your life, Mrs. O'Malley?"

"You betcha, Mr. O'Malley!" Carly said, and kissed him.

"That's *Lieutenant* O'Malley to you, *Mrs.* O'Malley." He pointed at the bugle on his uniform.

Epilogue

Carly was curled up on the sofa, her hands wrapped around a mug of hot chocolate as she stared into the fire. Adam had lit it earlier that evening in the living room of Becky and Will's former residence in Spruce Lake.

During the summer, Becky and Will had moved into the home Jack built for them on the ranchland Will had bought years ago, when he'd been an extreme-ski movie star. He'd subdivided it into large ranchettes. Matt and Beth already lived there, and next spring, Jack would start building a home for Adam and Carly.

But right now, her children loved the old Victorian and so did Molly. She was stretched out on Adam's blanket in front of the fire, snoring gently.

After seeing how happy Molly was with the O'Malleys, Mr. and Mrs. Polinski had decided that they wouldn't take her with them to the Twilight Years, after all. They'd asked Carly to keep her, as previously arranged. Since Molly missed hanging out with the ranch dogs now that they'd moved to town, Carly and Adam had adopted a companion for her from the pound.

Pongo was a dog of indeterminate breed, with over-size paws, floppy ears, a loud bark and a constantly wagging tail. Still a pup, he grew alarmingly each day and was completely devoted to his new family. He slept on Alex's bed every night and got up at odd hours to patrol the house, as if some instinct told him this family needed his protection.

Carly and Adam had repeated their wedding vows in the presence of all the children and Carly's parents a week after their hurried nuptials. Carly had felt blessed every day since.

"Whatcha thinking about?" Adam asked, plopping down beside her.

Carly smiled and leaned in to kiss her husband. "How much my life has changed this past year. How much better it is than it's ever been."

He kissed her back. "Mine, too."

"I don't think you thought that the first time we met."

"True. I had 'issues,' as Sash would say. But you healed me," he said.

"You healed yourself, Adam. You confronted your demons."

"You made me do it."

"Yeah, I'm good at twisting you around my little finger."

That earned her a tickle and then some playful wrestling that had Carly squealing and begging him to stop.

"The children!" she warned.

Adam sobered. "Speaking of children, would you be averse to having one more?"

Carly grinned. "*Another* O'Malley?"

"Just one."

Carly felt that having Adam's child would make her own happiness even more complete. "When can we start trying?"

"How about tonight?"

"Goodness, you *are* eager!"

"Well, you're not getting any younger," he teased.

"May I remind you, Adam O'Malley," she said, shaking her finger at him, "that I once punched out an ornery stallion. So don't mess with me."

Adam nuzzled her neck. Carly could feel her indignation abate as he moved to her mouth and kissed her. She sighed against his lips.

"Mom and Dad would be thrilled with another grandbaby."

"They're already getting two more additions to the O'Malley clan next year," Carly said, referring to Beth and Becky, who were both expecting babies in the spring. "Three in one year might be overkill."

"Never!" Adam declared. "Besides, with the birth of little Isabelle last month, Luke's said he and Megan aren't having any more kids, so Mom's been dropping hints."

"We could adopt another dog instead."

Adam laughed. "Then this place would be a complete madhouse! How about a cat?"

He reached for the latest copy of the local paper resting on the coffee table and turned to the section where the animal shelter advertised pets for adoption. "There's a litter of kittens here—"

"Hoo, boy!"

"Calm down, sweetheart. I called the shelter today and they've all been adopted. However, the mom needs a home."

Carly kissed him. "You are such a sweet man."

"I'm a firefighter, I'm not allowed to be sweet!"

"But you are, and I love you for it. Can we get her first thing in the morning?"

"Sure, the kids would have to come along, though."

"They'd want to adopt every animal there!"

"Good point. I'll go by myself and have Mrs. Farquar make up a special box, gift wrap it and I'll bring her home in that. She'll be a one-day-early Christmas present for the kids."

"You're the world's best father," Carly said. "Of kids, dogs…and cats."

"My brothers might argue with you about that, since they think they're so good at fatherhood."

"Speaking of fatherhood, what are we going to do about Jack? He'd make a fantastic dad. But we need to find him a wife first," Carly said. "I wonder what sort of woman he's attracted to?"

"Hard to say. He keeps his private life private."

"Like someone else I once knew," Carly murmured with a smile.

Adam ignored her jibe. "He had a huge crush on a really neat girl in high school, but she went off to college on the East Coast. Broke his heart."

"Is that why he entered the seminary?"

"Don't know. Not sure why he left it, either," Adam said pensively.

"You've never asked?"

"No. Now, can we forget about Jack's love life and concentrate on ours?"

"What's the holdup?" Carly said, wrapping her arms around his neck.

Adam hoisted her easily into his arms and headed toward the stairs.

Molly looked up sleepily, smiled—Carly was sure of it—then snuggled deep into her blanket and closed her eyes.

* * * * *

HEART & HOME

COMING NEXT MONTH
AVAILABLE APRIL 10, 2012

#1397 BABY'S FIRST HOMECOMING
Mustang Valley
Cathy McDavid

A year after Sierra Powell gave her baby up for adoption, little Jamie was returned to her. Determined to make a new life for both of them, she returns to Mustang Valley to reunite with her estranged family. But she doesn't expect to run into Clay Duvall, a former enemy of the Powells...and the secret father of her son.

#1398 THE MARSHAL'S PRIZE
Undercover Heroes
Rebecca Winters

#1399 TAMED BY A TEXAN
Hill Country Heroes
Tanya Michaels

#1400 THE BABY DILEMMA
Safe Harbor Medical
Jacqueline Diamond

REQUEST YOUR FREE BOOKS!
2 FREE NOVELS PLUS 2 FREE GIFTS!

◆ Harlequin®

American ★ Romance®

LOVE, HOME & HAPPINESS

YES! Please send me 2 FREE Harlequin® American Romance® novels and my 2 FREE gifts (gifts are worth about $10). After receiving them, if I don't wish to receive any more books, I can return the shipping statement marked "cancel." If I don't cancel, I will receive 4 brand-new novels every month and be billed just $4.49 per book in the U.S. or $5.24 per book in Canada. That's a saving of at least 14% off the cover price! It's quite a bargain! Shipping and handling is just 50¢ per book in the U.S. and 75¢ per book in Canada.* I understand that accepting the 2 free books and gifts places me under no obligation to buy anything. I can always return a shipment and cancel at any time. Even if I never buy another book, the two free books and gifts are mine to keep forever.

154/354 HDN FEP2

Name _____ (PLEASE PRINT) _____

Address _____ Apt. #

City _____ State/Prov. _____ Zip/Postal Code

Signature (if under 18, a parent or guardian must sign)

Mail to the **Reader Service:**
IN U.S.A.: P.O. Box 1867, Buffalo, NY 14240-1867
IN CANADA: P.O. Box 609, Fort Erie, Ontario L2A 5X3

Not valid for current subscribers to Harlequin American Romance books.

Want to try two free books from another line?
Call 1-800-873-8635 or visit www.ReaderService.com.

* Terms and prices subject to change without notice. Prices do not include applicable taxes. Sales tax applicable in N.Y. Canadian residents will be charged applicable taxes. Offer not valid in Quebec. This offer is limited to one order per household. All orders subject to credit approval. Credit or debit balances in a customer's account(s) may be offset by any other outstanding balance owed by or to the customer. Please allow 4 to 6 weeks for delivery. Offer available while quantities last.

Your Privacy—The Reader Service is committed to protecting your privacy. Our Privacy Policy is available online at www.ReaderService.com or upon request from the Reader Service.

We make a portion of our mailing list available to reputable third parties that offer products we believe may interest you. If you prefer that we not exchange your name with third parties, or if you wish to clarify or modify your communication preferences, please visit us at www.ReaderService.com/consumerschoice or write to us at Reader Service Preference Service, P.O. Box 9062, Buffalo, NY 14269. Include your complete name and address.

HARI1B

Get swept away with a brand-new miniseries
by USA TODAY *bestselling author*

MARGARET WAY

The Langdon Dynasty

Amelia Norton knows that in order to embrace her future,
she must first face her past. As she unravels her family's secrets,
she is forced to turn to gorgeous cattleman Dev Langdon for
support—the man she vowed never to fall for again.

Against the haze of the sweltering Australian heat Mel's
guarded exterior begins to crumble...and Dev will do
whatever it takes to convince his childhood sweetheart
to be his bride.

THE CATTLE KING'S BRIDE

Available April 2012

And look for

ARGENTINIAN IN THE OUTBACK

Coming in May 2012

Taft Bowman knew he'd ruined any chance he'd had for happiness with Laura Pendleton when he drove her away years ago...and into the arms of another man, thousands of miles away. Now she was back, a widow with two small children...and despite himself, he was starting to believe in second chances.

Harlequin Special® Edition® presents a new installment in USA TODAY bestselling author RaeAnne Thayne's miniseries,
THE COWBOYS OF COLD CREEK.

Enjoy a sneak peek of
A COLD CREEK REUNION

Available April 2012 from Harlequin® Special Edition®

A younger woman stood there, and from this distance he had only a strange impression, as though she was somehow standing on an island of calm amid the chaos of the scene, the flashing lights of the emergency vehicles, shouts between his crew members, the excited buzz of the crowd.

And then the woman turned and he just about tripped over a snaking fire hose somebody shouldn't have left there.

Laura.

He froze, and for the first time in fifteen years as a firefighter, he forgot about the incident, his mission, just what the hell he was doing here.

Laura.

Ten years. He hadn't seen her in all that time, since the week before their wedding when she had given him back his ring and left town. Not just town. She had left the whole damn country, as if she couldn't run far enough to get away from him.

Some part of him desperately wanted to think he had made some kind of mistake. It couldn't be her. That was just some other slender woman with a long sweep of honey-blond hair and big, blue, unforgettable eyes. But no. It was definitely Laura. Sweet and lovely.

Not his.

He was going to have to go over there and talk to her. He didn't want to. He wanted to stand there and pretend he hadn't seen her. But he was the fire chief. He couldn't hide out just because he had a painful history with the daughter of the property owner.

Sometimes he hated his job.

Will Taft and Laura be able to make the years recede...or is the gulf between them too broad to ever cross?

Find out in
A COLD CREEK REUNION
Available April 2012 from Harlequin® Special Edition®
wherever books are sold.

Celebrate the 30th anniversary
of Harlequin® Special Edition® with a bonus story
included in each Special Edition® book in April!

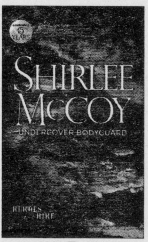

Harlequin *Blaze*™
red-hot reads

Sizzling fairy tales
to make every fantasy come true!

Fan-favorite authors
Tori Carrington and Kate Hoffmann
bring readers

Blazing Bedtime Stories, Volume VI

MAID FOR HIM...

Successful businessman Kieran Morrison doesn't dare hope for
a big catch when he goes fishing. But when he wakes up one
night to find a beautiful woman seemingly unconscious on the
deck of his sailboat, he lands one bigger than he could ever
have imagined by way of mermaid Daphne Moore.
But is she real? Or just a fantasy?

OFF THE BEATEN PATH

Greta Adler and Alex Hansen have been friends for seven years.
So when Greta agrees to accompany Alex at a mountain retreat
owned by a client, she doesn't realize that Alex has a different
path he wants their relationshiop to take.
But will Greta follow his lead?

Available April 2012 wherever books are sold.